ALSO BY RENA MASON

The Evolutionist

RENA MASON

EAST END GIRLS

This is a work of fiction. All of the characters, names, incidents, organizations, and dialogue in this novel are either the products of the author's imagination or are used fictitiously.

EAST END GIRLS
Copyright © 2013-2020 by Rena Mason
ISBN: 9798630342546

Cover © 2020 by Lynne Hansen | LynneHansenArt.com
Interior design by Todd Keisling | Dullington Design Co.

All rights reserved. No part of this book may be used or reproduced by any means, graphic, electronic, or mechanical, including photocopying, recording, taping or by any information storage retrieval system without the written permission of the publisher except in the case of brief quotations embodied in critical articles and reviews.

The views expressed in this work are solely those of the author and do not necessarily reflect the views of the publisher, and the publisher hereby disclaims any responsibility for them.

for Rob, Gehret, and Parker

—the West End Boys

AUTHOR'S NOTE

From August to November in 1888, five women were brutally murdered in London's East End that were attributed to Jack the Ripper because of their MO. There were also two murders that some speculate could have been his "starter kills." One occurred in the spring of 1888, and the other in the summer of the same year. Mary Kelly was his last victim and most vicious murder in London. Many people believe that he came to America and began butchering women in a similar style to the ones in Whitechapel. Reports came from New York City beginning in the spring of 1889. The bodies of women being found murdered in very much the same way Jack's victims had been. These reports continued across the United States all the way to San Francisco for over more than a decade.

Since then, there have been hundreds of books written about Jack the Ripper—Who he was, why he murdered those women and then seemingly stopped, if it was possible he was a *she*, and even that he was an alien from another planet. Could it have been Royalty? Perhaps a conspiracy? The point is, regardless of all the theories, these murders remain some of the most remembered and written about crimes in history.

"It is the same woman, I know, for she is always creeping, and most women do not creep by daylight."
— *Charlotte Perkins Gilman*

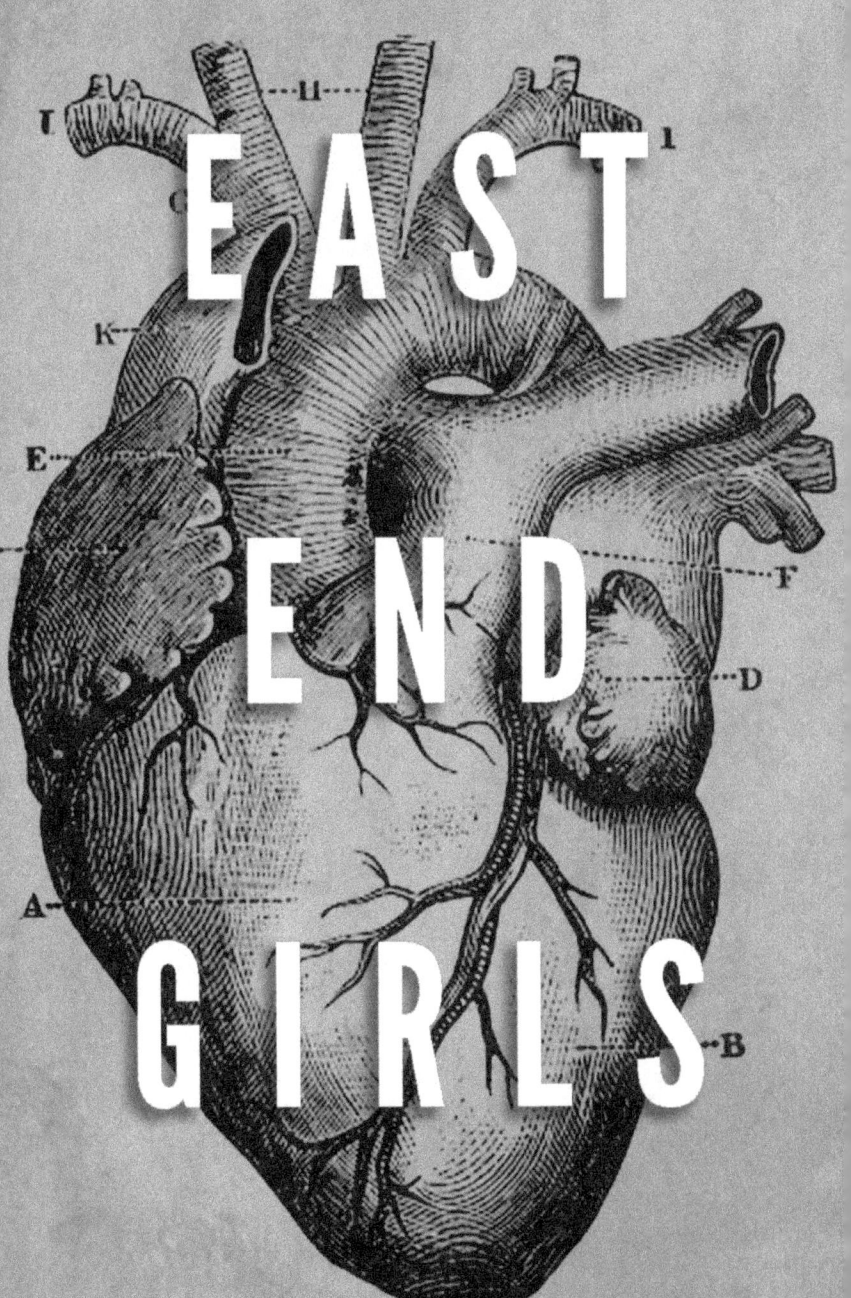

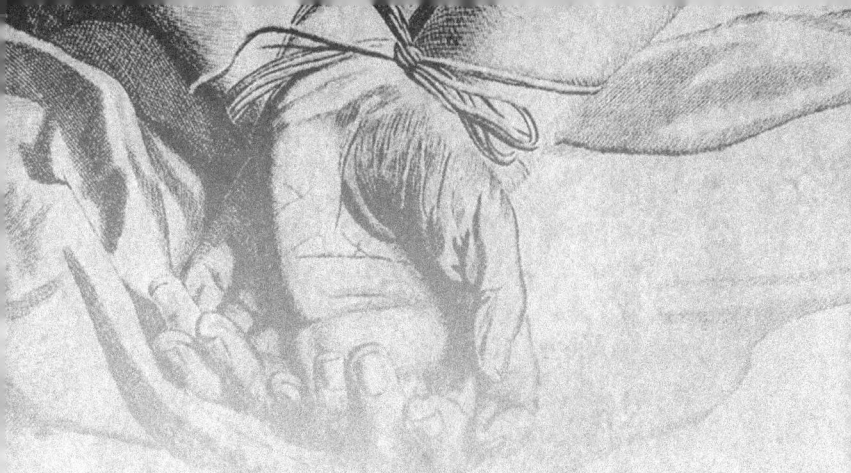

CHAPTER 1

Steam rose from Eliza's gloves as hot blood continued to gush out of the wailing prostitute. "For the love of God, hold her still," Eliza said to the prostitute's friend, who nodded and strengthened her grip. "It'll be the end of us if a copper hears." *The end of me anyway, my life, and good family name.*

She had been christened Catherine Elizabeth Covington on June 3, 1870. Her parents, Lord and Lady Covington of Northumberland call her Eliza, but the East End prostitutes knew her simply as 'Jane.' Where or how she got the nickname, Eliza never learned or cared to find out.

It was times such as this that made her wonder why she was wearing a hooded cape like a villain, kneeling in a back alley of the loathsome Whitechapel District with her hands between the legs of someone so far beneath her both metaphorically and literally. Then she would remind herself it was in pursuit of finishing up at the London School of

Medicine for Women to become a physician like her father, and this thought alone was enough to keep her going. Eliza dreamt of being the first female doctor to care for a member of the Royal Family. Why not? Times were changing fast, and she was ready to do whatever it required to see her dream realized—even despicable things such as what she was doing now. The vile creatures of the East End had been a way to advance her knowledge, and they got something out of Eliza's charity and studies, too.

The uterine curette had slipped from Eliza's grasp and she'd inched her fingers further up inside the harlot in search of the bulbous metal handle. The other end was shaped into an open oval.

Sharp around all its edges, the instrument was perfect for scraping the inside of a uterus. The woman squealed and clamped her legs together, making the task more difficult.

"Keep her calm," Eliza said, looking up and around for anyone who might be passing by.

The woman repositioned her hands on her friend's legs, held them firm, and then spread them farther apart. "You sure you know what you're doin' Miss Jane? Seems a lot of blood for such a little thing."

The prostitute patient began squirming again.

"It's perfectly normal," Eliza said. "But there would be less of it if she were to just keep still!"

The friend turned her head toward the patient and whispered. "Be calm now. She'll be done soon enough."

Up to her elbow in filth, Eliza thought of the mess that would be left on the sleeve of her frock coat. Granted, it was one she wore specifically for university and these ventures in the East End to blend with the residents of the area, but still, she would have to wash most of it herself before handing it off to the servants. She knew choosing a black one would be smart, because she *was* smart and of superior intelligence regardless of what Professor Huxley had to say. He could go hang himself.

"I got it." Eliza said. With a firm grip on the handle, she roughly circled the instrument inside the prostitute one last time, then she pulled it out. A warm gush of bubbling crimson and gore followed.

"Ugh," the friend leaned away and gagged. "It's done then?" "Yes. She should rest for the night." Eliza said.

"I'll make sure of it Miss Jane. And er…I ain't got nothing to pay for your services, less you want a little piece of me." The woman smiled, exposing her yellow teeth and furrowing the dried dirt caked over her brow and on her cheeks.

"That won't be necessary, but see to it this doesn't happen again." Eliza pulled strips of fabric from her medical bag and stuffed them into the patient's vagina using the curette she had removed a moment earlier. She'd been stealing the servants' undergarments and shredding them for just this purpose over the last few months, and if any of them had noticed, they'd never mention a thing about it to her. Eliza knew it was a very clever idea—*superior intelligence*.

"I swear this dollymop won't be seeing the likes of 'ya again, Miss Jane."

"That goes for you, too."

"You know I got experience compared to her. Not like me to get knocked up."

"Fine then." Eliza stood, looked around to be sure she had all her things.

"And what about that mess on the ground between her legs?" "Clean it up or leave it. I'll have no part."

"And the pieces? What am I to do with those?"

"Scoop them up and get rid of them. Here's some cloth." Eliza unlatched her medical bag once more and handed the prostitute a larger swatch of fabric. "Burn it all if you can."

Eliza stepped into the fog and made haste.

London haze in general was abysmal, but the murk that permeated the East End was rife with smoke and a wretched stench of the poor. A few blind turns past derelicts and common people coming and going from whatever business occupied them and soon the more familiar look of Wentworth Street would come into view. The busier thoroughfare would make it possible for her to catch a hansom cab back to London Hospital. During the ride, she would remove her cape and frock coat, change her shoes and tidy up. When Eliza was really a mess, she'd go into the hospital and wash before taking another cab from the hospital back home to Queen Anne Street, near Regent's Park. Until then, she was fortunate the despicable fog hid her from the police and criminals alike.

Some nights she would walk along the wet, rugged cobblestones and ponder her future, which appeared dimmer than the East End lamplights that were useless in the fog, their glow seemingly miles away. Her wedding, set to take place in several months to Sir Osborne's son, Henry, however, felt close enough to smother her. As dismal as the walks in the area were, the people of the East End had an unexplainable energy about them that was missing from her own life, and she envied it. So many East Enders had a bad criminal nature and without a care. It seemed hardly fair sneaking around to further her education.

If I became a vile, loathsome creature, the East End would welcome me into its bosom.

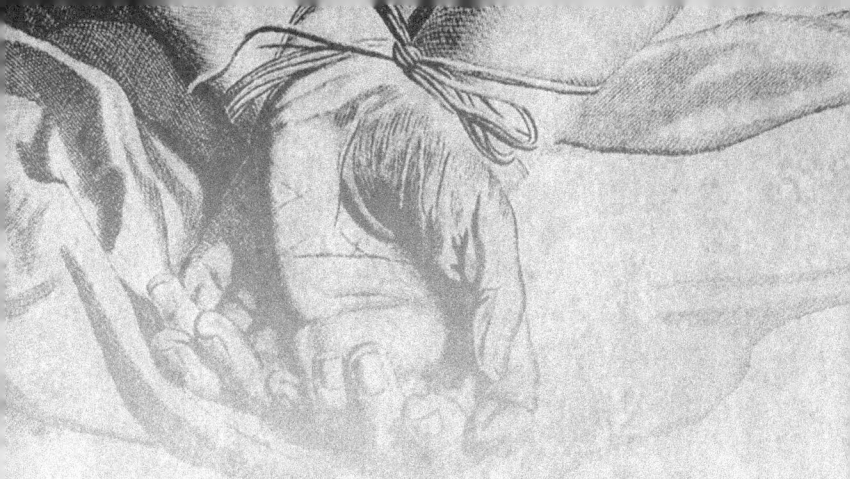

CHAPTER 2

ecause of the hour, Eliza used the servants' entrance when she arrived home. It also gave her the opportunity to rinse the sleeves of her frock coat and cape before exchanging them with Margaret for a plate of cold supper. Margaret was married to Mr. Daniel Sutton, the Covington's butler. Together the couple took charge of the other servants and gardeners.

After dining, Eliza visited her father in his study and poured him a glass of his favorite brandy. It had been a nightly tradition since she could remember. As a young girl, Eliza wanted so much to understand his work, be a part of it. She was fascinated by his knowledge of medicine and his dedication to the Royal Family. If any of them fell ill or were injured, he was called for at all hours, even if he was exhausted after seeing other patients all day. A phaeton carriage would arrive and be waiting outside to speed him away. There were quite a few physicians that cared for royalty, but it was well-known that Lord Covington was one of Queen Victoria's favorites.

However, it wasn't until Eliza showed medical interests in her later studies that Lord Covington finally took notice of her pursuits and approved. Since then, they would spend hours at night discussing new procedures, illnesses, and medicine in general. Nothing made her happier.

This evening was different, though. The air was heavy and grave as Eliza approached her father's study. She could hear other men in the room, so she gently leaned against the door to listen. Their voices boomed and vibrated through the solid mahogany, but she couldn't discern any of the conversation. No longer able to stand it, she rapped on the door with her fist.

"Who is it?" Lord Covington asked.

"It's me, Father. Can I come in?" Eliza could hear some protest from the men in the room. "Is that Henry in there with you?"

"Come in, Eliza," her father said.

She turned the knob so quickly she almost fell into the room. "Close the door behind you. We wouldn't want your mother to hear. Gentlemen, this is my daughter, Eliza."

Two men quickly stood from chairs by the fireplace.

"Eliza, this is a colleague and old friend from my university days you've never met, Doctor Rees Llewellyn." His name was said with great reverence. "And this is Detective Sergeant George Godley." His introduction was made with little to no sentiment. "Please gentlemen, continue. Don't let her looks fool you. More than likely, she's brighter than the three of us together."

"But sir," the detective said.

"That's Lord Covington to you, Godley."

"Gentlemen, please," Eliza said. Seemed she came at the right time. Eliza walked over to the brandy tray, poured some into a snifter then brought it to her father who was seated at his desk. He acknowledged her with a nod and they stared into each other's sky blue eyes for a moment, his expressing seriousness and hers curiosity.

Eliza turned her head toward Detective Godley and Doctor Llewellyn. "Would either one of you care for some brandy?"

"No thank you, Miss. We're here on business," Detective Godley said.

"Quite the beauty she is," Doctor Llewellyn said. "I hear congratulations are in order, Miss Eliza."

She looked up at him with no idea of what he meant. For a moment she thought perhaps her father had told him about her progress toward becoming a physician.

"For your upcoming nuptials to Henry Osborne," he said.

"Oh yes, thank you doctor." She sat down and made herself comfortable in a high-backed chair next to her father's desk. For several moments, the rustling of her starched skirts, the occasional crackle from the fire, and Godley's labored breathing were all that could be heard.

"Come now gentlemen, let's get on with it. We haven't all night," Lord Covington said. "We're discussing murder, Eliza."

Detective Godley gasped. The shortness of breath suited him. He was a stout man stuffed into an old jacket that was far too small. The plaid, tan vest underneath was pulled so tight, it protruded his rotund belly. The man's face was flushed, and his hair, black as night, was matted to his head with some kind of cheap tonic that reeked of wet animal.

Doctor Llewellyn, who was tall and lean in comparison, turned to face her. "A few women have been found with their throats slit this summer at the East End. But this last one...this last one had her abdomen cut as well." When he spoke, his face appeared worn, as though he'd had a rough life. But otherwise, he was clean-shaven, and his dark blue suit was kempt. He looked much older than her father did, even though he had said they'd been university colleagues.

"They think perhaps this fiend is evolving, Eliza," Lord Covington said. "It happened near the London Hospital." He gave her a stern look, but mentioned nothing to the men of the volunteer work she sometimes did there. Fortunately, her father knew nil of the loathsome deeds she endured in order to learn the female anatomy, for he would never approve.

"Are you certain it is the same murderer?" she asked. Detective Godley gasped again and plopped himself down into a chair. The color in his face had gone, and he was quite pale. Doctor Llewellyn walked over to the brandy tray and poured some into a glass. He stepped over to the detective and handed it to him. "Drink this, Godley. For heaven's sake man, pull yourself together. This woman is practically a physician already from what I hear, and surely she's cut a few bodies open herself. We speak of nothing she hasn't done or seen."

Eliza glanced at her father and they both smirked. The detective took the glass with a shaky hand, downed the brandy in two hardy swallows, then handed the snifter back to Doctor Llewellyn.

"The cuts are always the same," Doctor Llewellyn said. "From left to right."

"So either your villain is left-handed, or he gets at them from behind," Eliza said.

"See, Rees, I told you she was sharp," said Lord Covington. Doctor Llewellyn raised the empty glass in his hand and nodded at his colleague. "That is correct, Miss Covington."

"Was there anything else, besides the abdominal cut?" she asked.

"She had been drinking and was probably strangled first. There was little blood loss at the scene. Her innards were protruding from the open wound, and there were numerous slashes crisscrossing her abdomen," Doctor Llewellyn continued.

Detective Godley began coughing. Then he stood upright. "Please, sirs, and lady," he said. "You'll have to excuse me. I've been feeling a bit under the weather."

Doctor Llewellyn took the detective's empty glass and set it down next to the brandy tray. "Yes, it is getting late. I suppose we've overstayed our welcome."

Lord Covington rose from his desk. "It was good to see you again Rees after all these years. Don't be a stranger. I'll be sure to have Lady Covington add you to the wedding party, and please consider joining us for Michaelmas."

"Thank you, Thomas. Please give my regards to Lady Covington. And if you can think of anything else that might help with the case...or even you for that matter, Miss Eliza," he turned toward her and bowed slightly. "Do send us a message. But I'm hoping this is the end of it. I look forward to seeing you again in September under more celebratory circumstances."

"Until then, Rees," said Lord Covington. He came out from behind his desk and shook hands with Doctor Llewellyn.

"It was a pleasure to meet you both," Eliza said.

"The pleasure was all ours young lady." Doctor Llewellyn raised her hand to his lips and kissed it gently.

Detective Godley stood by the door, looking a bit green in the face. He held up his hat. "Good evening Lord Covington. Miss Eliza."

Godley opened the door and Mr. Sutton, the butler, who'd been waiting just outside the study, motioned for the two men to follow him out.

Eliza walked over and shut the door after they went. "Father, why haven't I met Dr. Llewellyn until now? Does Mother know him? You've never mentioned him before."

"He was a good friend at University, but he had some problems his last year. Got addicted to laudanum from what I heard. It was a sad business, too. Rees was one of the brightest students who ever walked those halls. Seems he pulled through after the rest of us had finished up and moved on. Was never able to recover his reputation, though."

"Why was he here with the detective?"

"He's a police surgeon now."

"What a shame," Eliza said.

"Indeed." Lord Covington looked over to his wall of books and appeared to study them for a moment. "I don't want you anywhere near London Hospital in the evenings. It's too dangerous."

"But Father, I'm only there twice a week, and I have my wits about me."

"I know that, but it's of little help when there's a maniac on the loose."

"It sounds like he's after drunken East End girls anyway, not medical volunteers who help the sick and the poor."

"I won't speak any further on this subject, Eliza. You are not permitted to go to the East End. I will have a meeting with Professor Huxley and that Ms. Anderson first thing tomorrow."

She lowered her head, turned around, and started for the door. "Is there anything else you'd like to say to me young lady?"

"Good night, Father."

"Good night," he said. His tone softened. "You'll see that it's in your best interest to stay away. Besides, your mother has been blaming me for keeping you from your wedding plans. Henry's a good man, Eliza. He'll make a good husband."

"Yes, Father." A single tear rolled onto her cheek as she opened the door and stepped out of the room. Months ago, he was in full support of her attending university and all the work that went with it. She couldn't understand why a few murders now would make him change his mind. People died in the East End all the time. It wasn't unusual to have a body floating in the Thames there at least every other day. No, it couldn't be that her father was so worried about it. This change of heart must be because of her mother. Eliza's familial and social commitments would be the death of her. There had to be a way of escaping them, and she was desperate to find it.

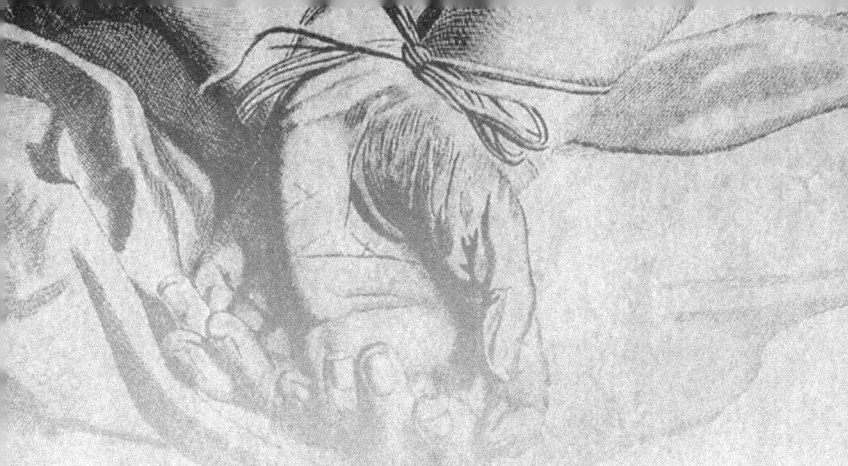

CHAPTER 3

t breakfast, Lady Covington was alone when Eliza came into the room. "Where's Father?" she said.

"He told me he had to leave early and speak to Professor Huxley this morning."

"Oh." Eliza sat down. Mrs. Sutton appeared with a plate of toast with jam, and a cup of tea with a bit of milk. "Thank you," Eliza said.

"You're welcome, Miss Eliza. Did you sleep well? You look a bit pale this morning."

"I slept fine."

"She's right," Lady Covington said. "You don't look so well. Maybe you should stay home today."

"I could have Mr. Sutton send a note to Professor Huxley," Mrs. Sutton said.

"You can rest and I'll show you what I've chosen for the silks, the flowers, and the—"

"I'll be leaving as soon as I finish my tea, Mother. I assure you, I am quite well."

"You speak to me the way your father does."

Mrs. Sutton quickly exited the room.

"Well, I am his daughter."

"I won't have it, Eliza. I've been burdened with the details of your wedding these past few months and a bit of help now and then would go a long way. A young girl your age should be happy to be marrying a man from a good family and with future prospects."

"Yes, but—"

"Not running around all over London attending university, laboring as if you were a man, and God only knows what else. It's not proper, don't you understand? You're fortunate Henry tolerates it and loves you enough to allow you this whim, but be sure that when the wedding is over you will be doing your duty as his wife, not doctoring anyone but him."

Eliza clenched her fist and slammed the butter knife onto the table.

"It's all such a waste of time," her mother continued. "Why can't you see it? You are so much like your father it's hardly tolerable."

"Well Mother, you won't have to take too much more. I'll soon be married, away, and out of your hair for good."

"Don't be that way, Eliza."

Eliza knew there was no point in arguing with her mother. After years of watching her father lose battles it was obvious neither of them would ever win one. "I'm sorry Mother, it's just that exams are coming up and there's so much to study for. Regardless of whether or not Henry lets me practice doctoring, I'm determined to finish my studies."

"Yes dear. I understand. It's just that…"

"What is it, Mother?"

"It's Ann Williams, dear. She's been out of sorts lately and I really wish you would see her more often. You two used to get along so well. I worry for her health."

"I've been a little busy, and I'm sure she understands."

"Please, promise me you'll call on her soon. The last time I saw her out, she seemed dire."

"I'll visit her in the next few days, I promise." Eliza swallowed the last bit of her tea and placed the delicate china cup on the table.

Mrs. Sutton came back into the room. "Shall I have Mr. Sutton ready the carriage?"

"I'd much rather take a hansom."

"Now you're being ridiculous," said Lady Covington. "These new ideas of yours are preposterous. You can't tell me every girl there doesn't already know who you are."

"It makes no difference. I'd still prefer a cab."

"Be home early today. Henry's joining us for dinner. It'll do you good to see him and maybe he can talk some sense into you."

Lady Covington was ringing the bell for Mrs. Sutton again when Eliza rose from the table and left the room. She put on a hat before stepping out of the house, and made sure everything she needed was in her medical bag. Outside, Eliza looked up the street and saw the Williams's home at the crest of the hill. It had been a while since she'd spoken to Ann. Eliza truly hoped she was all right, but it would have to wait.

The most important days of her life were coming, and nothing would distract her from her studies. Too much depended on it.

"Miss Covington, would you please point out the deceased's fallopian tubes," Professor Huxley said with a sharp tone. His voice echoed and bounced off the cold, stone walls until the words seemed to come from the cadaver itself. She could feel his dark, beady eyes glaring at her through his wire-rimmed spectacles. He was awkwardly tall and thin with a tendency to lean over and watch her work, intimidating her whenever the opportunity arose, as now.

Eliza looked down and saw a swirling puzzle of bluish-purple innards. "Here, sir." Thinking herself clever knowing there are two ovaries, she pointed to one thing and then to another on the opposite side which looked similar.

"If we were to have it your way Miss Covington, women would not be able to reproduce. Those are arteries of the kidneys. Your knowledge, or rather, lack thereof, astounds me. I suggest you study up on the subject," he whispered over her.

"Yes, Professor Huxley," she said. The heat of embarrassment flushed her face. Before she could retort, he'd moved on to the next student, taking away her opportunity. Eliza hated her lack of a quick wit.

The classmate, Jessica Blake, was always ready with her correct answers. They were all just jealous, but being made a fool of wasn't something she was familiar with or would ever get used to. Between her parents, Professor Huxley, and even Henry, it would be a feat if she ever accomplished anything other than marrying a good man. But, like she'd told herself so many times before—one had to stay determined in order to succeed.

After class, she approached the professor when all the other girls had left. "Professor Huxley, may I have a moment?"

"Yes. What is it Miss Covington?"

"My father, did he—"

"Yes, Lord Covington paid me a visit this morning."

"And you told him…"

"I told him you were excelling in all the facets of doctoring, Miss Covington. I may be a simple professor of medicine at a university for *females*, but I am no ignoramus as to my position and rank in society."

"Did he mention London Hospital?"

"Yes, it seems you are no longer permitted to go there in the evenings. I didn't have the courage to tell him that you were never assigned to volunteer there at those hours. I do admire your determination Miss Covington, but you should take care in your extracurricular means of study. I can promise you that you will graduate from this university and then be married to Henry Osborne, after which you can finally give up the notion of being a medical doctor. It will give me great peace, and I will be able to sleep at night knowing you are not out there practicing any kind of medicine, on any living person. Good day, Miss Covington." Professor Huxley turned around and walked away from Eliza.

She stood in the center of the room unable to move for some time after hearing Huxley's harsh words. Eliza leaned against the wooden table where the cadaver was earlier. It was the only thing keeping her upright for the moment. The sun crossed a high window, moving a slow shadow across her face, and she finally snapped out of the trance. It was time to get home and dress for dinner. Henry would be there and if nothing else, perhaps he could cheer her up. Give her a bit of good news after Professor Huxley's extreme display of discontent. Eliza knew she wasn't the smartest girl at the school, but she didn't think she was the most ignorant either. It was imperative she get more practice in at the East End. She would have to be very clever to keep it from her parents and extremely sharp to stay away from a possible madman on the loose. It was a challenge she felt up for.

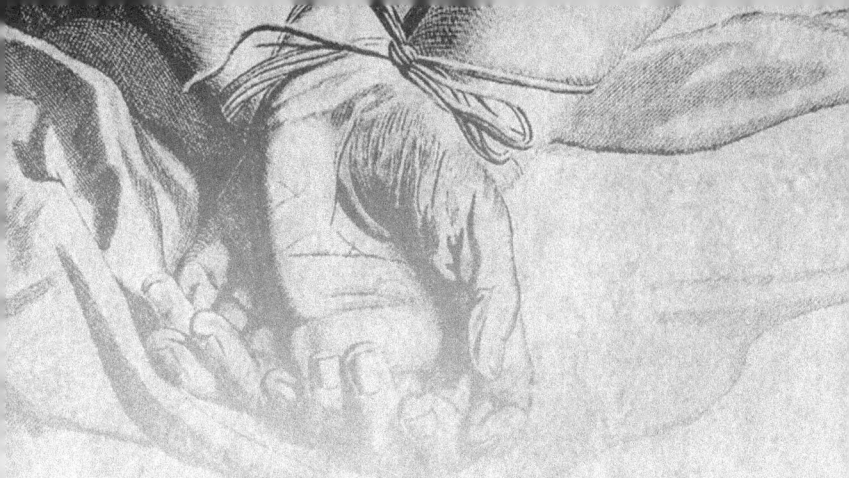

CHAPTER 4

Eliza couldn't sit still and kept rearranging the silverware around her plate. During the meal, she continuously sneaked glances at Henry, who looked dashing in a fashionable new navy pinstripe jacket. She'd already told him several times since he'd arrived how handsome he was, and her mother couldn't have agreed more. Her father, however, told him he looked quite ridiculous—but he'd always been more on the conservative side of fashion.

The jacket wasn't the reason she was so excited. It was Henry announcing why he'd worn the jacket. Right before dinner, he said he wore it to tell them about some especially good news after the meal. Henry was a handsome young man with brown hair he kept neatly slicked back and a thin moustache. Eliza didn't like his eyes, though. They were brown and narrow, making him look as though he were always keeping something secret. Regardless, she could hardly wait to hear what he had to say.

"Please Henry, what news?" she whispered into his ear. Before moving away, she gently breathed down his neck.

His smile grew wicked. "Clever girl, are you trying to seduce me?"

"Is it working?"

"Father's always told me I'm good at keeping secrets, and I'm not about to give this one up."

"Not even for me?"

"You'll be my wife soon, and then there will be nothing kept hidden between us." He raised his glass and took a sip of wine while staring into her eyes.

Eliza knew that what he'd said wasn't true. Henry was a man's man, all about business. His father, Sir Osborne, was a banking magnate in London. It was well known that the patriarch of the Osborne fortune had numerous affairs with other women all throughout England and even Paris. Henry was every bit like his father, and he'd most likely behave in the same manner. A husband's infidelity was almost expected. But why, she'd never understand.

The world was changing. Women wanted rights and were getting them. The poor wanted rights now, too. Parliament was in an upheaval over it. The conditions at East End were inhumane, and in these times of rapid modifications, it shouldn't be fair that men could still cheat. But some things Eliza knew would never change and this made her angry.

She thought of her good friend in the house on the hill, Ann Williams. The last time Eliza spoke with her, Ann was still upset over her inability to have children. She had also hinted that she thought her husband might be having an affair. Maybe this was why Lady Covington wanted Eliza to visit with her so badly. Although she seemed quiet and demure, and in her own way really did care, her mother had an insatiable penchant for gossip.

Finally, dinner had ended and everyone gathered in the parlor afterwards to hear Henry's announcement. Even Mr. and Mrs. Sutton found an excuse to come in and stay longer, rearranging dessert plates around on the sideboard table. Henry sat next to Eliza and then stood when Lord Covington entered the room. Beads of sweat formed on Henry's upper lip and he couldn't stop rubbing his hands together. Eliza couldn't remember if she'd ever seen him like that before, not even when he asked her father for her hand in marriage. The suspense was astounding—and giving her a headache. She hoped he would say whatever it was soon so that she could excuse herself and get some rest.

"Please, Henry, sit," Lord Covington said.

"I'd rather stand if you don't mind, sir. This is big news."

"Well, get on with it then lad, before you explode. Eliza looks as if she might faint."

Eliza looked up at Henry and rolled her eyes then smiled to give him some encouragement.

"As you all know I'll be taking over the business when my father retires, but..."

Eliza took hold of his hand. He squeezed her fingers and continued. "He is sending me to New York City, in America, to establish one of our banks—and there it is."

The room went quiet. Eliza pulled her hand from his grip and let it drop onto the chaise. Her father was right; she might faint after all. Lady Covington let out a high-pitched whimpering sound like a wounded cat. Mrs. Sutton gasped and knocked over a crystal goblet of water. Mr. Sutton hurried over to help her clean up the mess.

"Well," Lord Covington broke the silence, walked over to Henry and shook his hand. "Congratulations, son. No doubt you'll be off right after the wedding."

Lady Covington mewled again.

Eliza stared straight ahead, and Henry, trying to catch her eye responded, "Yes, of course. I wouldn't think of leaving London without my wife, Eliza. I've waited long enough to have her hand in marriage. Our engagement has been extended more than most."

The word wife suddenly triggered hatred within her. She wouldn't be a good one. He deserved someone better. She had to speak up. "But my education, Henry, it would all have been for nothing there."

Lady Covington stopped squealing and glared across the room at Eliza. It was as if little pins shot out of her eyes and pricked Eliza all over.

Henry sat down and took Eliza's hands into his. "Oh my dear, there will be so much for you to see and experience in America, you may forget about wanting to be a doctor." She tried to pull her hands from his, but he held tight. This was an aggressive side of Henry she hadn't noticed before. "But there are universities there for women, as well. If you really have your heart set, I'm sure there are places where you can practice medicine."

Eliza knew he was lying, but there was nothing she could say.

It was what her mother wanted to hear, and Henry knew it.

"See Eliza, there's still hope after all," her father said. There was a deceitful tone in his voice, and for the first time in her 21 years, she saw the man's man side of her father. Eliza couldn't believe what she was hearing and wanted to run out of the room screaming.

"Yes," she said, her lie coming as quickly as his. "That would be wonderful, Henry." Then she leaned up and gave him a peck on the cheek.

Mr. and Mrs. Sutton left the room with the wet linens. Her father stood.

"Come on now, Henry, let's leave these women to their chatter." The men left for Lord Covington's study to drink brandy and smoke cigars. Despite how angry she was at the both of them, Eliza wished she were there—anywhere but alone in a room with her mother.

"You truly will be leaving me soon." Lady Covington began to whimper. "What am I to do with my only child gone? And so far away."

"If you don't mind, Mother, I have a bit of a headache. I think I'll go upstairs and retire early this evening."

"You do look pale, dear. I don't blame you for feeling ill with such news. I think I should be happy, but I'm feeling quite sad. Will you let Mrs. Sutton know I'll be retiring early as well?"

Eliza rose from the chaise, walked over and kissed her mother on the forehead. Lady Covington grabbed Eliza's hand and kissed it. "Oh, my little girl," she cried.

For the third time this evening, Eliza pulled her hand away from someone and walked out of the room. A part of her was numb—another felt dark and enraged.

CHAPTER 5

Nearly a month later, Eliza still felt dull and out of sorts about the idea of moving to America after the wedding. The uncertainty drove her hard into her studies, and she was more determined than ever before. There were more late nights spent at the Royal Free Hospital, plus daytime volunteer work, all in addition to her curriculum. She took whatever work she could to improve her medical knowledge, but it still wasn't enough. Eliza knew she needed the East End. It needed her, and she wanted it. All she had to do was walk the streets with her medical bag in hand, and she would be approached by the sick or injured and sometimes by prostitutes hoping she could take care of their business in the back alleys they were so accustomed to. If she was going to be forced to live a life she didn't want, she would first do what she could and learn as much as possible in the East End.

It was late when Eliza snuck out. She had to be certain everyone was asleep. With her bag under her arm, she walked as far as she could from the house before taking a hansom to Whitechapel. The fog was so thick she could hardly see the cab driver. By the time she got there, it had started to rain. Eliza pulled the hood of her cloak over her head and kept her bag slightly open in case she needed to reach in for a weapon. Wet and cold, she stood by a building prostitutes frequented, and waited. Raindrops pitter-pattered against the tin roofs around her. Chimney smoke from the workhouses and homes of the poor blackened the fog, making it look green in the dim lamplights. Every breath inhaled was poison, so she folded the bottom part of her hood over her mouth.

After a few minutes, she heard muted footsteps. The water and haze distorted sounds, and Eliza couldn't tell from which way they came. She reached into her bag and carefully felt around for the handle of her surgeon's knife. Nimble fingers searched out the smooth mahogany, sized for a man's hand. The blade end was the same length, made of durable, sharp stainless steel. Against an attacker, the surgeon's knife would be a menacing weapon. She was happy to have it in her bag; a gift from her father. It wasn't long before she was approached.

Two women, drunk as she'd ever seen anyone, stumbled up and nearly knocked her over. "Sorry miss," one said while brushing off Eliza's cape with filthy hands. She had dark hair and a plump face compared to the other woman, who was rail thin; both were obviously working women.

"See you got a medical bag there, Miss. You wouldn't happen to be called Jane, would ya?" the one with the long scrawny face asked.

"I am."

"Good. Ah…Emma here's got a little problem she needs you to take care of." The prostitute patted Emma's belly and giggled.

"Do you have a doss for the night?" Eliza said. "A room is best to do the work."

"No miss, we spent it on drink. Besides, looks like the rain's lettin' up."

"Is there any place else?"

"Right around the corner will do. Emma here's not picky. Not a lot of folks out this time of night."

"Fine then, let's get to it." Eliza walked about 20 yards until a street pump for water caught her attention. This would be good for cleaning up afterward, so she turned left and walked down a long corridor behind a three-story building that was partially lit up from a lamplight in the rear yard. She figured it was as good a place as any, and she would have plenty of room to work. Two small outbuildings weren't too far off in the back yard and she hoped one was a lavatory where things could be discarded. "Lie down here," Eliza told the prostitute, Emma. "Use the bottom doorstep to rest your head. Help her—what's your name?" she asked the other prostitute.

"Catherine, miss," she slurred, then belched.

"Not your real name!" Emma scolded.

Catherine shrugged her shoulders and both women giggled.

"Keep your voices down, or I'll leave this minute!" Eliza said.

Catherine looked properly chastised. Eliza often wondered why these stupid, disgusting animals worried so much about using their real names. She didn't care one way or the other who they were because it was unlikely she'd ever see them again. "We must keep quiet unless you want trouble from the tenants."

Once they had Emma positioned correctly, Eliza lifted the prostitute's skirts and readied her instruments. First, she took out a piece of wood wrapped in cloth that was a little longer than a finger and just as thick. "Here," she told Emma. "Bite down on this to keep quiet when the pain comes." Emma nodded and put the stick in her mouth.

Eliza pulled down the woman's filthy drawers. She left her gloves on and inserted two fingers deep into Emma's vagina while pressing the woman's abdomen with her other hand. She was sure she felt a lump that wouldn't normally be there. The patient grunted and her musculature stiffened. "Try and calm her," Eliza told Catherine. "It will make things go easier."

While Catherine patted her friend's head and whispered everything would be all right, Eliza pulled the long curette from her bag and slowly inserted it into Emma. The woman wriggled and bucked like a wild animal and her friend was worthless at holding her still. Emma bit down hard and grunted, swinging her head back and forth. Tears streamed across her temples. "I can't do this," Catherine said. She got up and ran off with her hands over her mouth. Eliza heard the prostitute's footfalls tap loud and quick at first, then they grew faint, until they faded to nothing.

"Don't worry," Eliza told Emma. "We don't need her, but you've got to hold still."

Emma nodded and Eliza continued circling the curette. She grabbed another instrument with a sharp hook at the end, inserted it, and pulled when she felt it had caught on something. Emma's eyes bulged and she screamed with the bit still in her mouth. "Almost done," Eliza said. She yanked hard and a glob of tissue came out with a rush of bubbled blood that reeked of feces. "Dammit," Eliza said, knowing she'd hit bowel.

Emma began to scream louder and louder. Eliza was in a panic, didn't know what to do. She thought first of what Professor Huxley would say. He would tell everyone he knew she was a horrible surgeon. Her father would be so disappointed. Her mother would be ashamed, and Henry would never take her as his wife. Eliza leaned forward and tried to shush Emma, pinning her arms to her sides to keep her from flailing about. They struggled, and when that didn't work, she grabbed hold of the sides of the bit in her mouth and pushed down. Emma freed herself and reached into her pockets for something. Eliza grabbed her hands, tore the fabric of Emma's dress, and loose junk from the pocket flew up into the air then landed scattered about. Emma tried to fight. Eliza twisted up the scarf Emma had around her neck and began choking her, used her thumbs to push hard against her trachea until Emma passed out. Crazed, Eliza searched in her bag for the surgeon's knife. She held it up and stared at the glinting blade just as Emma started coming to.

Eliza leaned over her body then used the scarf to turn her head to the right. With little life left in her, Emma didn't put up much of a fight when Eliza took the surgeon's knife and cut across her throat from left to right. Eliza let go of the handkerchief and quickly began her work down below. There couldn't be any evidence left behind and she would have to move fast.

It was fortunate she'd been there to hear the details Dr. Llewellyn gave when he and Detective Godley came to visit her father—almost as though it was meant to be. And her own father gave her the best bit of advice. If the killer was evolving, then this would be his next step. Taking a thing—a prize.

Eliza opened Emma up and heaped her innards on top of her chest to get to the uterus. It had to go. Everything that could lead back to this failed abortion had to be taken and discarded. The extraction took less than a quarter of an hour. Then she wrapped the uterus and other parts of incriminating evidence, into a large swatch of fabric from her bag and tied it off with a piece of string. Quietly, but very alert, she went up to the front of the building, set the organs down next to the water pump and rinsed her hands off best she could. It started to rain again. Eliza put the bundle into her bag and hurriedly walked down the street. Every footstep was a loud splash against stone. She caught a hansom cab that delivered her close to Regent's Park, where she got out and walked the rest of the way. Eliza clutched her medical bag hard against her chest as though it might open and spill out her horrible secret.

When she got home, Eliza used the servants' entrance, went down into the kitchen, took the bundle from her bag and placed it onto the fire along with her gloves. The flames grew to life with her offering, but she added two more logs to be sure.

EAST END GIRLS

Her hands wouldn't stop shaking. What if the police don't believe my cover-up? That won't, and can't happen. Before anyone in the house woke up, Eliza rinsed her cape and frock coat best she could then went upstairs to change for breakfast.

Despite all the feelings roiling inside, hunger rose above all else.

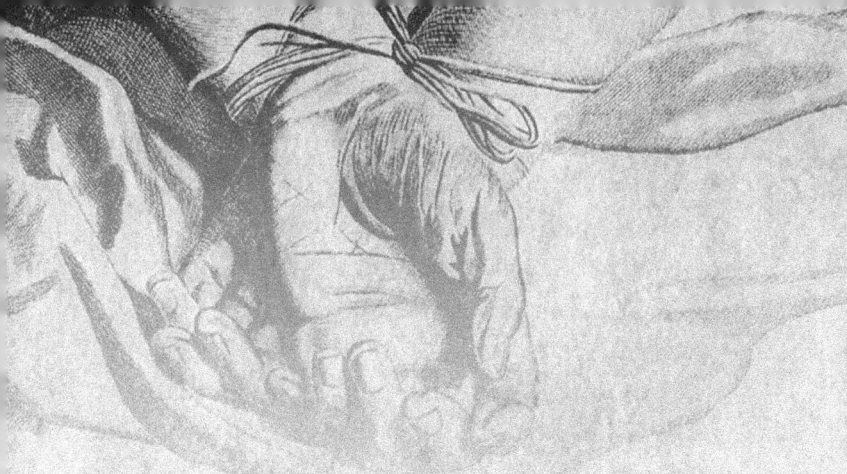

CHAPTER 6

"You look flushed this morning, Eliza. Are you feeling all right?" Lady Covington said.

"The other day I was too pale, and now I'm flushed. Are you sure it isn't your eyes?" Eliza sat down at the table and thanked Mrs. Sutton for a cup of tea.

"That's no way to speak to your mother," Lord Covington said.

"See how she treats me, Thomas?"

Eliza rolled her eyes. "Oh Mother, you know I don't mean it."

"Then don't vex me like that," Lady Covington said. "After church will you go over the flower arrangements with me?"

"I can't today. I'm playing tennis with Henry, Henrietta, and her husband, Arthur."

"How is his sister getting along since her marriage?" "I've not heard much about it."

"That's because you've got your nose in books all day. It

would be to your advantage after your own wedding to listen to what's happening in society."

"But I don't really care what happens with society." "You will when it pertains to your husband, dear."

"Ladies, please, might a man have a piece of toast without the bickering?"

Mrs. Sutton entered the room, placed fresh jams on the table and set a folded paper down next to Lord Covington. "I thought you might like this right away, sir." He nodded. Then she stepped over to Eliza and poured more tea. The maid leaned over and whispered in her ear. "Nanette says your frock coat and cape are soaking wet. What would you have her do?"

"Wash them," Eliza said. "I decided to walk home yesterday and got caught in the pouring rain."

"Yes, Miss."

"Did you say you walked in the rain yesterday?"

"Yes, Mother." Eliza watched and waited for her father to open the paper.

"Are you trying to catch a death of a cold?"

"No, Mother. What news, Father?"

He looked up from the paper. "Walking is a healthy thing," he said. "It's good exercise."

"Yes, but in the rain, Thomas?"

"Well, maybe when it's pouring out take a cab next time, Eliza." He went back to reading the paper. "Hmm...seems there's been another murder in Whitechapel."

"That's horrible," Eliza's mother said. "Must we discuss this while we eat?"

"Thank you, Father," Eliza said. "May I be excused to dress for church?"

"Yes, you may."

Eliza took the stairs down toward the basement washroom and found Nanette, one of her best servant girls, standing over a large wash basin. Eliza picked up a can of soap on the shelf next to her and threw it against the wall in front of the maid. White powder exploded everywhere and the young girl screamed and turned around.

"Was there a problem with my coats, Nanette?" Eliza said with clenched fists.

"No, Miss, they were just so wet and heavy like they'd been left outside in the rain. They smelled funny, too. I thought that perhaps you'd want to throw them out." The maid trembled and rattled off her words.

"You know those are the clothes I wear to school and to work in."

"Yes, Miss."

"Well, they'll have to do until I'm finished then, won't they?" "I'm sorry, Miss."

"Don't be sorry, Nanette. I'm a bit out of sorts this morning, that's all. Please, just wash the clothes when I bring them to you, with no comments to Mrs. Sutton or anyone else. Do you understand?"

"Yes, Miss."

"Then hurry up and clean this mess before someone sees, and don't tell a soul what happened here, either." Eliza walked upstairs and dressed for church. No doubt the news of the murder had spread throughout all of London. She meticulously scanned over images in her mind regarding the night's event. Eliza could think of nothing she might have forgot or left at the scene in her rush to clean up and leave.

During the entire sermon, she kept her eyes down and thought of the other prostitute, Catherine. What if she told someone? Eliza doubted a woman of her nature would go to the police. Still, she would have to find her somehow and figure out a way to strike a bargain to her keep quiet.

A match or two of tennis would help her think things through. Her mind was always more clear when she was active. Sitting stagnant in church with her mind running in circles did nothing to help. It was suffocating, which made her think of the grip she'd had on Emma's scarf when she was strangling the girl. Her hold had been firm; so much so, she could hardly believe her own strength. Eliza moved her hand over her bicep muscle and marveled at the definition in her arm. All the tennis matches and archery competitions had made her stronger than she realized. She looked up from the pew and smiled.

Henry took Eliza home in his phaeton carriage and she wondered where her heart was. Would she ever fall in love with him? Her mother told her it would come with time, but shouldn't she feel the least bit for him now? *Love and marriage are useless things. Life and death, those are real.*

Eliza knew that once she became a fully-pledged physician she'd have some control over what was real. But losing control, like she did last night, had also been liberating. This kind of freedom without conscience could get her into a great deal of trouble. She had to be careful. Perhaps someone at the Royal Free Hospital would know of a prostitute named Catherine.

"What occupies your thoughts so, Eliza? Say it's me."

"Of course it is." Eliza was pleased with her increasing ability to lie so easily. "You, our wedding, our future lives in America."

"I hope you'll be happy, dear."

"I'm sure I will."

"Good. Good."

Henry's driver brought the carriage to a halt in front of the Covington residence then helped Eliza step out. "I'll see you soon," Henry said from the door.

"Goodbye, Henry."

Eliza sensed unease when she walked through the front door. She removed her hat and gloves. Mrs. Sutton came into the foyer and took the items from her. "Lady Covington would like to speak with you."

"Is there someone else here?"

The maid looked from one side to the next then whispered. "More detectives and the police surgeon have come again. Something to do with the Whitechapel Murderer, I presume."

Eliza started for her father's study.

"Miss Covington, your mother is waiting for you in the parlor."

"Yes, of course, but—"

"Trust me when I say you wouldn't want to be in the same room with that severe bunch. Even your father looks more stark than usual. Best you be on your way to see what Lady Covington requires."

"Thank you Mrs. Sutton." Eliza headed for the parlor, slowing her pace when she passed her father's study. Men's voices boomed through the closed doors, making Eliza's heart race. Perhaps they'd caught on, which hastened her steps. If anyone knew what was happening in the house, it would be her mother.

"There you are, Eliza. Where have you been?"

"I told you earlier Mother, with Henry playing tennis."

"Oh, yes, now I remember. These events have me so distraught I hardly know what to think. It's horrible of these men to keep your father from his dinner. A man needs his nourishment, and he's not getting any younger or healthier."

"Mother, it's important. They need his help." "His help? Why on earth do they need his help?" "Well, he's esteemed, Mother. They trust him." "I suppose, but it is very inconvenient."

"Who is here speaking with him? Are they the same men from before?"

"How would I know?"

"Mother, you must have some idea."

"I can't believe you're more concerned about what is going on in that room full of men than the reason I called you here."

"All right, why did you send for me?"

"The dressmaker is coming tomorrow afternoon."

"Oh, mother, how can you think of such things when father is in his study talking to detectives about murder?"

Lady Covington raised her voice. "If I don't, it will be your wedding day, and you'll be walking up the aisle in your nightclothes. What is murder to humiliation? I won't have it. You need to be home early tomorrow for the dressmaker, and I'll have no more talk of death or detectives."

"Yes, mother." Eliza had never seen her so upset. No sense

in vexing her any further. At least she could be at ease knowing none of them suspected she was guilty of murdering a prostitute. If they had, she was certain her mother would have mentioned it.

Dinner was served late that evening, and Lady Covington made sure to tell everyone she suffered from a cruel headache, so most of the conversation centered on her health. After pudding, Lord Covington returned to his study and Eliza followed. She could no longer contain her curiosity. The door was barely closed when she spoke. "Father, please tell me, what news of the Whitechapel Murders?"

Lord Covington furrowed his brow. "You shouldn't concern yourself with these matters; although I can tell you that I knew this kind of thing would only get worse. They've got Inspector Abberline on it now. Expect to have it wrapped up soon."

"He's that good?"

"I've never heard anything other than exceptional remarks about him."

"Hmm..."

"What is it? You seem a bit out of sorts. Your mother again?"

"I have to be home early tomorrow to meet the dressmaker."

"Is it all that bad? You are getting married soon."

"No, that's not it."

"Second thoughts are normal. You'll get over it eventually, and you know I'd love nothing more than to have you practicing next to me. But as it is, I'm up half the night listening to your mother worry about your future."

"I'll be fine."

"Truly?"

"Yes, Father. Goodnight." Eliza went around the desk, leaned in and kissed his cheek. He looked more tired tonight than usual. She was sure his mind was occupied with thoughts on how to catch a madman, and so she did not want to keep him from his bit of solitary peace and quiet.

In her room, Eliza noticed her cape and frock coat hanging over the cabinet door of the armoire. Nanette had done a good job getting them clean. Eliza sighed. She'd be unable to walk the East End tomorrow in search of the prostitute, Catherine, but at least there'd be time to ask around the Royal Free Hospital. Degenerates from many London districts came there at one point or another for care. Someone was bound to know of one or two women named Catherine.

She hoped.

CHAPTER 7

Professor Huxley stood in the center of the room with a scalpel in one hand and the decapitated head of a man in the other. He made a circular incision around one of the cadaver's eye sockets then set the blade down on the table. "Move in closer, ladies. Mr. Smith here won't bite. He just wants to get a better look at you is all."

Everyone stepped in while Professor Huxley dug his fingers into the dead man's orbit. There were wet slushy sounds as he moved his digits about. When he pulled the eyeball out, it made a small pop. He proceeded to walk around with the head and the eyeball, showing everyone the ocular nerve and muscles.

All this time and the professor still continued to try and elicit some form of dramatic reaction from the women in class—perhaps with the hope some of them might change their minds. None of them would. They were all determined, just maybe not as much as Eliza, but who knew. Maybe she didn't give them enough credit. The university accepted students from near and far and from every walk of life. *Anyone* could apply, which was why her mother had been so against it. But the world needed more female physicians who understood and cared about the human condition as well as physiology and pharmacology. Doctoring encompassed so many facets of life, and Eliza knew she had what it took to be one of the best. Nothing would stop her from obtaining that goal. The title would earn her respect among her peers. Maybe other high society women would take notice and try to further their education. It wasn't enough to be a lady from a good family who was destined to marry well. Not anymore. Times were changing.

After class, Eliza gathered her things and left the schoolhouse on Handel Street in search of a hansom cab to ride home. As she walked past the side of the old red brick building, she felt as though someone down the alleyway, between buildings, was watching her. Moving quickly and often looking behind her, Eliza had the sense of being followed and stalked. When she finally hailed a cab, it had never been such a relief to get in one. Eliza knocked on the underside of the roof with her fist to get the driver moving. As soon as they rounded the corner, she felt safe again. The sensation of being watched left her. She sat back and sighed in relief, and wondered if it was her imagination. Who would wish to seek her out? Then she thought of her father and the detectives. Perhaps they were having her followed for safety reasons. She wouldn't put it past her father. It couldn't possibly be because they suspected her.

EAST END GIRLS

Upon arriving home, then entering her mother's parlor, Eliza had stepped back in time. Long panels of glorious white and ivory silks and laces were strewn across every piece of furniture. Strands of pearls and sparkling beads hung from the backs of chairs. Having gowns custom-made and sewn by hand was a regal indulgence. In an era when too many clothing factories were popping up and putting out ready-to-wear attire, and most ladies of society were traveling to Paris for their gowns and wedding clothes, superior London seamstresses such as Mrs. Plympton, were becoming more rare with each passing year. The Covingtons would never use anyone else, and her father insisted on spending their money in England. They preferred traditional methods and Eliza supported their ideas wholeheartedly.

"Good afternoon, Miss. It's good to see you again." Mrs. Plympton stepped up and shook hands with Eliza.

"What took you so long? We've been waiting nearly an hour," Lady Covington said from across the room.

Eliza rolled her eyes and Mrs. Plympton smiled. "Shall we get started then?" the seamstress said. "Oh my, what a lovely broach."

She reached her hand up and gently touched it.

"It's my great grandmother's."

"Will you be wearing it on your wedding day? I can design a special place for it on the neckline with some small ruffles encircling the piece, perhaps."

"That sounds lovely, Mrs. Plympton."

The broach was a bouquet of flowers made of fancy-cut

diamonds and pearls. Eliza received it from her mother for her sixteenth birthday. The party was a glorious affair. *Hard to believe that was only two years ago.*

With the help of Mrs. Sutton, who was already there eyeing the fabrics, Eliza removed all her clothing except for her corset and drawers. Lady Covington sat in her favorite chaise, sipping tea, and nibbling on biscuits in between ordering everyone around.

"Your daughter has a very muscular build, Lady Covington," Mrs. Plympton said, sounding slightly shocked. She measured the length of Eliza's arms and legs, her waist, and every other part of her body with a measuring tape she uncoiled from an ivory case.

Lady Covington rose from the chaise to have a look. She put her hand around the bicep muscle of Eliza's right arm. "It appears you're right, Mrs. Plympton. What have you been doing girl, rowing boats down the river?"

"Tennis, Mother. And the archery events, when I can attend."

"Eliza is quite the archer, Mrs. Plympton. She has several winning pins. Tennis offers no such trophies," Lady Covington said the latter with less enthusiasm. She'd never been a fan of Eliza playing lawn tennis, always said it was much too physical a sport for a lady.

"Indeed, more active women tend to have bigger muscles." "This won't affect the sleeves of her gown will it?"

"Not at all, Lady Covington, unless she carries a bouquet of iron flowers down the aisle."

"That is not the least bit amusing, Mrs. Plympton. You don't know how I've toiled over this wedding. I've done nothing but plan, organize, and worry for months. My daughter here shows no interest, and it wouldn't surprise me the slightest if she were to carry iron flowers."

"Is that so? Why do you put the task all on your mother?" Mrs. Plympton asked Eliza.

Lady Covington pulled a lace-edged handkerchief from up her sleeve and used it to dab her forehead as though she were overworked and perspiring. Eliza couldn't think of a time when she ever saw her mother do a bit of work, so the act was ridiculous and typically overdramatic. "Ouch," Eliza said. One of Mrs. Plympton's pins had stuck into her side a bit.

"Sorry," Mrs. Plympton said.

Lady Covington walked back over to the chaise and sat down. "You've known my mother for years now, Mrs. Plympton,"

Eliza said in a soft voice.

"Why yes, nearly two decades."

"Then you of all people should know my mother has been planning this wedding for all that time."

Mrs. Plympton giggled and quickly put her hand over her mouth. When she was done, she went back to draping and pinning. "How right you are, Miss."

"I am simply my mother's daughter."

"Well said. And what's this I hear about you going off to America after the wedding?"

"It's true. Henry's father wants him to start up one of their banking establishments."

"I'm sure you'll be fine."

"It's not England, though. I will miss...everything." Eliza sighed.

"I'm sure you will."

With the mood turned melancholy, Mrs. Plympton began chatting with Lady Covington about some of the other ladies in town. Eliza stared off into space, her mind empty of thought.

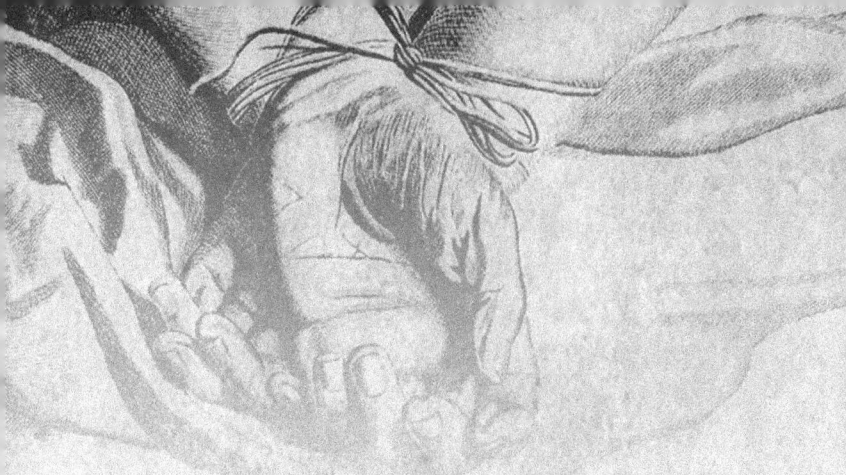

CHAPTER 8

Dinner was early at the Covington house. Eliza joined her father in the study afterward and they had hardly begun to discuss the day when Mr. Sutton knocked on the door to announce the arrival of Inspector Frederick Abberline and a Doctor George Phillips.

Two men entered the room and immediately removed their hats at the sight of Eliza. "Good evening, gentlemen," Lord Covington said. "I was sure to dine early this evening in case you came again. This is my daughter, Eliza."

The inspector gently shook hands with her as did the doctor. Then they stared at one another, then at Lord Covington, and then at Eliza.

"My daughter's studying to be a physician at the London School of Medicine for Women," Lord Covington said, when the silence grew awkward.

"Interesting," said Inspector Abberline. He was a portly man, like Detective Godley. What little hair he had was mix of red and gray. His moustache, beard, and sideburns were overly bushy as if to make up for the lack of it on top of his head. "Does she know of the murders in East End?" He said in a soft-spoken voice. The inspector's demeanor reminded Eliza of Henry's father, the banking magnate.

"Why don't you ask her?" Lord Covington said. He looked at her and winked.

"Well, Miss, have you thoughts on the Whitechapel killings?" "Yes, inspector."

"And do you think it's possible a woman could have had a hand in it?"

"Inspector!" Lord Covington said. "What are you suggesting?"

"Doctor Phillips and I think there's a slight possibility a midwife would have what it takes to dissect these women the way we've been finding them."

"The knowledge, yes," said Lord Covington, "but the strength? Just look at Eliza. She has the skills to perform surgeries, but under a different set of circumstances entirely. Her patients are anesthetized, sedated. Even a drunkard puts up a fight, and she hasn't the build."

"Unless the victim has blacked out," said Doctor Phillips.

"Let her speak," said the inspector. "Answer the question please, Miss."

"If they're already unconscious by strangulation," Eliza said. "Why bother stopping the job to slit their throats? It seems to me the perpetrator prefers to see the blood spilling out of his victims. More male in nature, I would think."

"Yes, I see your point. Thank you, Miss," the inspector said. He turned toward her father. "It was simply a theory, but after taking into consideration the barbaric nature of the crimes and the appearance of your daughter here, Lord Covington, I'm beginning to think it isn't possible. Her figure is so slight a strong wind might knock her over."

"Not all women are frail and weak, sir, no matter their physical appearance," Eliza said.

"Now this I know firsthand, Miss; my wife is neither one of those, but nor does she appear to be." All of the men roared with laughter. "However more masculine her figure may be compared to yours, Miss, she is also incapable of the heinous brutality exhibited by this madman."

"So, you are convinced the killer is a man now?" said Lord Covington.

"Yes, indeed I am."

"Good. Then the timing for your visit here was just right and my daughter's presence was to your benefit."

"It wouldn't be anything but, Lord Covington. Such a lovely girl." "Eliza, pour us some brandy if you please, and then leave us to the rest of the evening. I will catch up with you on your progress tomorrow."

"Yes, Father."

Eliza did as she was asked, and the men became more involved with conversations about the murderer. When Inspector Abberline mentioned that the most recent victim's name was Annie Chapman, Eliza was a bit surprised, yet her hand remained steady as she poured.

She listened closely while they surmised that perhaps it might be a butcher, maybe even a doctor. But then Lord Covington mentioned the Hippocratic Oath.

"That doesn't rule out a failed doctor," Abberline said,

and the others agreed with nods and 'ayes' that it was a possibility to consider.

Eliza left the room, relieved the inspector no longer had his sights on the possibility of a woman being the murderer. The next step was to find Catherine, the friend of Annie Chapman.

It was early afternoon when Eliza left the Royal Free Hospital. All week she sensed someone watching her, following her through the streets as she searched out a hansom. Eliza even started making the cab drivers take different routes and circle the park. Most of the time, it was only when she was on foot that she felt stalked. Still assuming it was someone her father had convinced to protect her, she did her best to ignore it.

Having time, Eliza took a cab to the London Hospital in East End to make some inquiries. After she paid the driver, Eliza pulled the hood of her cloak over and joined a crowd of factory workers heading back to work after their break. She walked past an open doorway and suddenly stopped when something inside caught her attention. The workers passed her by, and jostled her a bit as she stood there and stared at a blazing hearth fire. The image of a burning, sizzling uterus filled her vision, until someone inside closed the door. She blinked several times to clear the sight from her head then walked on.

Distracted by the grisly image, along with the feeling of being followed, Eliza inadvertently walked toward

Spitalfields, near where she had killed Annie Chapman. Unnerved by her choice of direction, she turned around on Thrawl Street and walked back toward London Hospital when a scruffy young boy ran up to her in a fit of hysterics. Eliza jumped back.

"Miss!" the boy said. "My mother needs help. It's a baby."
"Where?" The fear and panic in the boy's voice charged Eliza.

He started running back toward Spitalfields and Eliza followed, glad now she kept herself active with sports, despite her mother's protests.

They arrived at one of the small shanties that lined Brick Lane. The boy came to a wooden door that was nearly falling off its hinges, flung it wide open, and pulled Eliza in.

"Mum, please help."

There was a small cot in the corner of the room where a woman was lying, moaning, and rolling back and forth. Eliza hastily removed her cape and frock coat, threw them over a chair, and rolled up her sleeves. She went up to the bed and saw the woman's face frozen in what at first appeared to be a smile and then resolved into a grimace of pain as Eliza drew closer. The woman's hands clutched the bed sheets in a death grip. Beaded sweat covered her forehead and her nightgown appeared damp, clinging tight to her bulging pregnant belly.

"Boy! Run to the London Hospital as fast as you can and find a Doctor James Riley. Tell him..." *Tell him what? I can use my influence to help this woman, but father, I don't know...oh bloody hell!* "Tell him Miss Covington sent you to fetch him. He needs to bring a carriage. Go now!"

The boy ran and slammed the door shut on his way out.

The top hinge broke, and the door fell to one side leaving an open corner above. Eliza turned back to the woman and pulled the bed sheet down. Below the waist, her gown was soaked with blood, sweat, and amniotic fluid.

"What is your name?" Eliza said. There was a basin on a small table nearby.

"Louise," the woman said between grunts.

"Is this water clean?"

The woman nodded.

"How long has it been since the pain started?"

"'Bout three hours."

Eliza put her medical bag at the end of the cot and opened it. She pushed Louise's legs up, and they fell open and apart. "This is going to hurt," she said. "You will feel a lot of pressure. Try very hard to be still."

Louise nodded.

Eliza brought her fingers together into a point as best she could, then inserted them into Louise's vaginal opening. The woman let out a bloodcurdling scream that made Eliza see stars for a moment.

"Shush," Eliza said. "We don't want anyone barging in here thinking I'm hurting you. Pull the sheet up and bite down on it."

It didn't take long for her to feel the baby was breech. "Take quick short breaths," Eliza said. "That's good. And do *not* push. The baby's turned around." Eliza felt movement inside. "It's alive!"

Louise attempted a smile that quickly became a grimace, which was followed by a series of pants and grunts.

"I've got to rotate it," Eliza said. With her right hand still up inside the woman, she toppled her doctor's bag with her left hand and fingered through the items until she found a small leather case. Eliza popped it open and pulled a scalpel from its sheathed location. She looked up over the woman's belly to see her face. "I need to make a cut first. Brace yourself."

Eliza brought the scalpel forward and made an incision from where her forearm was inside Louise, nearly all the way down to her anus. The skin pulled apart and blood quickly filled the exposed area of open flesh. The woman screamed through the sheets and Eliza felt her pain—the pain only women seem to know and can relate to one another through.

"You're going to feel more pressure now," Eliza said as she pushed her other hand into Louise. She felt resistance. "Stop it! Don't push!" It let up and she continued.

Slowly, Eliza turned the baby until she felt its head. Louise was a hardy woman and did rather well considering Eliza was nearly up to her elbows with both hands and forearms inside her. She continued to scream, then grunt, and take quick short breaths.

"We're close," Eliza assured her, knowing she needed to work fast. She repositioned her hands and moved out just a bit. A contraction was beginning. "Push now, Louise. Push!"

The woman pushed, the contraction did its job, and Eliza had to pull the baby's head very little as her arms and hands were expelled from Louise's vagina, the infant right behind them.

Eliza caught the baby, held it up, and slapped it. When the newborn made its first wail, Louise let out a sigh and collapsed her legs onto the bed. Instruments in the open leather case at the foot of the bed flickered in the candlelight. Eliza pulled the case closer and removed a clamp. She put the umbilical cord between its metal teeth and brought them together. Then she took out a pair of scissors and cut the cord. It seemed she worked well under pressure, but she'd always known this. Delivering a breech baby was part common sense. *What do you do if a baby's positioned backwards? Turn it around.* Still, she was thankful for the midwifery classes at the university.

Louise tried to look up and see what Eliza was doing. For a moment, it was Annie Chapman's face she saw. Her eyes opened wide as saucers and she looked down expecting to see a bundle of gore in her arms, but instead saw the newborn. Eliza cut a clean piece of bed linen, wrapped it around the baby, and then handed it to the woman. "It's a girl," she said. "I've got to sew you up now."

Eliza stood and brought several more pieces of the cut bed linen over to the basin. As she wet the rags, the broken front door swung open on the one hinge and the boy barreled through it with Dr. James Riley close behind. "Thank goodness you're here at last," Eliza said.

"Looks like you've done just fine on your own."

"Yes, but..." Eliza thought about what to say. "I've got to get home, James. My father...I'm not allowed to be at London Hospital, the East End, because of the murders."

"And we've missed you very much." There was a slight smile on his face. Eliza knew he meant it. James had always been in love with her, but her father didn't approve. "But why—"

"Please, James. The baby was breech but I turned it around. She seems fine now. I was just going to sew her up. I thought she might need to go to the hospital."

"Don't worry about it. Take the carriage home."

"But how will you get back?"

"I'll walk, or take a hansom. You go on ahead."

"Oh thank you, James. You're a true friend."

He took a step closer to her. "It was good to see you again."

"And you too, James." Eliza leaned in and quickly pecked him on the cheek.

He smiled.

Eliza gathered her things and left without saying goodbye.

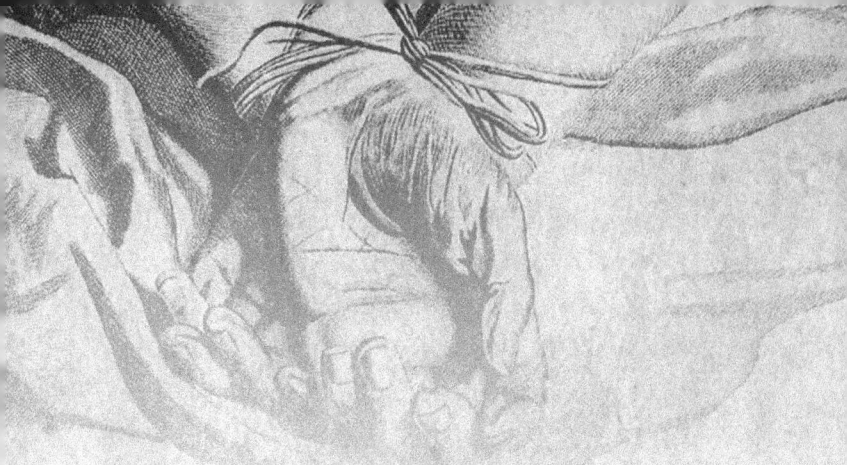

CHAPTER 9

liza couldn't get over her elation having just delivered a breech baby. The odds of that even happening and the infant surviving in the East End were staggering, but she'd done it. A part of her wanted so much to have the carriage stop at Henrietta Street so she could tell Professor Huxley, but she decided against it. The last thing she needed was anyone questioning why she'd been at East End, and she hoped James would not become a herald.

When Eliza arrived home, Mrs. Sutton met her in the foyer. "How was your day, Miss?"

"It was wonderful."

"Good to hear it. Your mother is in the parlor again and would like to speak with you."

"Can't it wait? I have to wash up."

"There's a man with her. They've been waiting a while."

"Please let them know they'll have to wait a little longer." Eliza huffed and headed upstairs.

She rushed cleaning up and changing, but was back downstairs within the hour. Before entering the parlor, she stood at the doorway and peeked into the room. A mousy looking bald man wearing thin-wired spectacles sat in the Queen Anne chair next to her mother's chaise. There was a large group of assorted floral arrangements on her mother's Chippendale table in front of them. Lady Covington looked up and saw Eliza.

"What are you doing over there creeping about? Come in here and meet Mr. Grey. He's going to be doing the flowers for Michaelmas dinner. And if we like them, he may very well do the arrangements for your wedding." The florist got up, an eager smile on his face, and Lady Covington rose from the chaise. Together they walked toward Eliza.

"Mr. William Grey," the man said, extending his hand. "Hello, Miss."

Eliza went to shake it, but Mr. Grey gasped and jerked his arm away.

"What is it?" Lady Covington said. She looked down at Eliza's fingers, which were still in midair. "Catherine Elizabeth!"

Dried blood had caked around the cuticles, underneath the fingernails, and in the wrinkles of her knuckles. "Oh forgive me." Eliza lowered her hand. "I was sure I got it all off." She ran out of the room, while Lady Covington yelled for Mrs. Sutton.

A while later, Eliza returned to the parlor and there was tea and a tray of biscuits in front of Mr. Grey. For the next hour, they spoke of nothing but flowers. Eliza had never met such a man before—squeamish of a little blood but so knowledgeable about everything botanical. If he hadn't reacted the way he did when he saw her hand, her mother would never have noticed. This made Eliza dislike him. Particularly while watching him nibble on the corners of the biscuits and sipping tea. *Exactly like a mouse.*

"Pardon me, Mother, may I be excused? I'd like to lie down a bit before dinner."

"Yes, of course."

"Goodbye Mr. Grey. It was nice meeting you."

He stood up when Eliza did. "It was my pleasure. Oh, and silly me, I nearly forgot to ask. Please, tell me, what are your favorite flowers?"

"Lilies," she said, "white ones." Mr. Grey stood there, his face pale with wide eyes.

Lady Covington huffed. "Silly girl," she said. "Don't mind her, Mr. Grey. She knows nothing of feminine things such as flowers."

"Those are for funerals," he muttered. Eliza turned to leave the room.

As much as Eliza wanted to speak with her father after dinner, she was exhausted, and took her meal upstairs. Mrs. Sutton was kind and sympathetic, adding a piece of her scrumptious pear tart to the tray.

After eating, she rested her head on a pillow and quickly fell asleep. Eliza dreamt she was walking in the East End and Annie Chapman was following her. The uterus Eliza had removed and burned was dragging just behind the prostitute, connected by an umbilical cord that came out from the bottom of her skirt hem. "You won't get away from me," Annie yelled. "You're a murderer!"

Eliza quickened her pace, but so did Annie. In her haste, Eliza tripped on a broken cobblestone and fell onto the wet filth that covered the street. Her hand landed in one of the cesspool puddles and splashed muck onto her face and into her mouth. A bitter-tasting grit stuck to her tongue, and she turned her head to the side and spat. The prostitute caught up to her and launched her body on top of Eliza's, pinning her down. Eliza struggled, and when she tried to call out for help, Annie grabbed the back of her head and pushed her face down into a puddle. Eliza fought harder, kicking and grabbing at the woman. Her skin stung from scraping against the abrasive pavement. Then Annie grabbed her by the shoulders and started shaking her violently, smashing Eliza's face against the foul, slimy wet ground.

"Wake up, Eliza! It's a bad dream." Her father's voice called out. She opened her eyes and saw his hands on her arms.

"Father," she cried. He pulled her close to him.

"Do you want to talk about it?"

"No." She sobbed into his shirt.

"I was just going to bed when I heard you screaming. Did you have a bad day?"

She shook her head. "I had a fabulous day. You would have been proud."

"I'm always proud, dear." He moved her away from him, and she lay back down in bed.

"Thank you, Father."

"Goodnight. We can talk about this in the morning if you like." Eliza nodded and closed her eyes.

This time, no nightmares of the dead invaded her sleep.

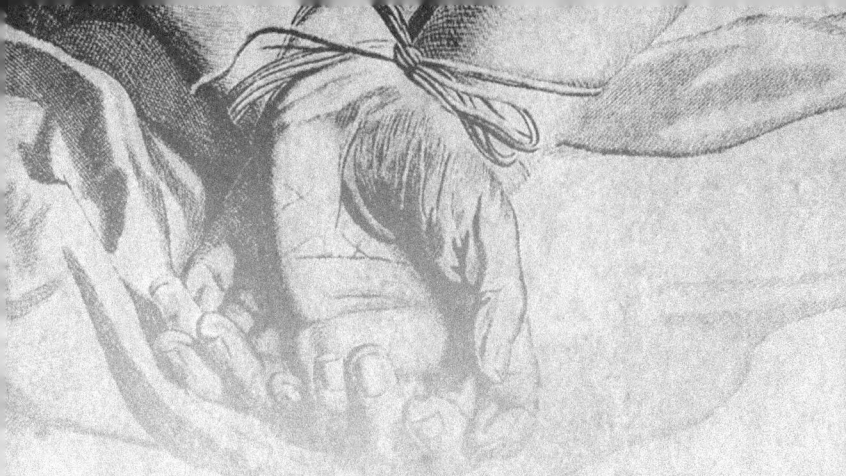

CHAPTER 10

Lord Covington wasn't at breakfast the next morning. "Where's father?" Eliza asked.

"He was called out very early."

"The Royal Family? Is someone ill?"

"I don't know the details. You'll have to ask your father."

"You look a little tired."

"Well, it's no wonder with his coming to bed so late then having to leave at all hours."

"Maybe you should take a nap."

Lady Covington sighed. "I suppose I will. For once I've a break from wedding planning."

"Then make good use of it. I'll try and come home early."

"It would be nice to have you home. You'll be leaving me soon."

"Please, don't start." Eliza downed her tea, grabbed her toast, and rose from her seat. "I've got to go."

Her mother was still talking when she went out to the foyer to put on her coat and grab the doctor's bag. Eliza made sure she'd had her cloak as well, hoping to try the London Hospital again if she finished before schedule. There was also the issue of talking to James about keeping quiet regarding what happened. Then she had the other prostitute, Catherine, to locate and take care of.

Despite the promise she'd made to her mother, she knew it was going to be a long day.

"Miss Covington, I heard news of someone delivering a breech baby at East End yesterday. Would you happen to know who that was?"

"Um...no, sir."

"I heard there were some great heroics and quick thinking involved."

"Indeed?"

Professor Huxley smiled and continued dissecting a cadaver spleen. Who would have thought the artery attached to it was so large?

At the end of class, the professor announced that three girls would soon be graduating. "Miss Blake, Miss Johnson, and Miss Covington will be moving on the latter part of this November." The rest of the women knocked on their books and cheered.

Eliza was in high spirits when she left Henrietta Street and took a hansom to the London Hospital at East End. So much so, she never noticed someone following her until, like in her nightmare, she stumbled on a broken cobblestone and fell onto her hands. This triggered the memory of the dream and a feeling of unease. Eliza looked behind her and caught a glimpse of a woman ducking into an alleyway. A couple of men walking by stopped and asked if she was all right, then helped her get back on her feet.

"I thought I saw someone down there." She pointed to the alley.

One of the men went to investigate. He walked halfway to the end. "No one here, Miss."

Feeling silly, she brushed herself off and thanked them, then went straight to the hospital.

Eliza greeted a few midwives and nurses she knew. "Where is Doctor Riley?" she asked Helen, one of the newer nurses.

"He's in C Ward, Miss."

"Thank you." Eliza headed to the area where they kept patients with breathing disorders.

Doctor Riley was writing in a patient chart when he turned and saw her walking toward him. He smiled and put the chart down. "I wasn't expecting to see you again so soon," he said.

"You didn't tell Professor Huxley did you?"

"Don't be upset."

"James, you—"

"Doctor Morton was the only person I told, and I swore him to secrecy."

"He's good friends with Professor Huxley. You knew that. How could you?"

"I had to tell somebody, Eliza. You were simply amazing."

"It *was* rather exciting news to keep quiet." She made a small smile. James was too innocent in his intentions to get distressed over. "Just promise me you'll tell no one else."

"I promise, and I don't think Huxley will say anything either. He's more afraid of your father than anyone I know. I'll never figure that one out."

"Father yelled at him once about a mistake he made regarding something he told a patient. Humiliated him essentially, and it hurt...practically ruined his reputation."

"Ah, that makes sense. Always wondered why a man would go into teaching women."

"James, you're horrible."

Doctor Riley laughed. "You know I'm teasing."

"Thank you again for coming to my rescue yesterday. It really meant a lot to me."

"You know I would've, I *would* do anything to help."

"I understand." Eliza leaned closer to him and kissed his cheek again.

"You really have to stop doing that, you know."

"Why?"

"It wrecks me for the next day or two."

"That's silly. Come on, I'll help you make rounds."

The two doctors worked side by side for the rest of the afternoon. Eliza used it as an opportunity to quietly ask patients she thought might be the street working type if they knew any women named Catherine, and she would give them a brief description. She didn't gain any leads, but she enjoyed her time spent with James. Eliza had forgotten how fond she was of him. When they'd finished seeing patients, James walked Eliza out and they said their goodbyes.

Outside, it had begun to rain. Eliza pulled her hood over and walked quickly down the street. She passed an alley and heard someone shout out. "Miss Jane!"

Eliza stepped back, looked up and down the street to see if she saw anyone she knew, then headed down the alley. Behind some wooden crates, a woman was huddled against the wall. "Can I help you?" Eliza said.

"I'm sure you can." The woman looked up at Eliza. At once, she knew that long rat face. It was Catherine. The prostitute was filthy, and smiling up at Eliza with a missing tooth and a blackened right eye.

"What do you want?"

"You've got to know. Lucky I didn't turn you in."

"Have you been following me?"

"You bet I have. Can't let my future slip away, if you know what I'm saying."

Eliza's heart began to race. This harlot knew where she came and went. "What exactly are you saying?"

"Don't play dumb with me, Miss. I want your money."

"I don't have any."

"You must have some! I've seen you take hansom after hansom. I was never able to follow you past East End. You could be heading home to Buckingham Palace for all I know. The one time I saw you on Henrietta Street I was taking a friend up to the Royal Free Hospital. She's all uppity these days and prefers it, and that's when I saw you leaving and followed you 'til you caught a hansom. So I'm smart enough to know you've got a lot of cab money, Miss." Catherine stopped talking. Her eyes targeted something on Eliza and then widened a bit.

Eliza looked down and saw her great grandmother's broach through the keyholes of her cloak and frock coat. Her heart sunk.

"That'll do," Catherine said with a wicked smile pointing to the broach.

Eliza gasped and tightened the cloak around her neck. "I can't. It's a family heirloom."

"I don't care whose family it belongs to. If you want me to keep quiet, you'll be giving that to me."

Unable to catch her breath, Eliza began to hyperventilate.

"Don't go faking sick on me. I'll scream out, I will."

"I'm not." Eliza gasped and tried to think quickly. She reached into her pocket and pulled out a small silk pouch with a drawstring. "Take this," she said. "It's all I've got."

"Why thank you, Miss." Catherine snatched the pouch out of her hand. "But I'll still be wanting that pretty pin."

"Please, not now, let me think about how I'll explain it going missing. It's my mother's. She only leant it to me. The excuse will have to be a good one because she'll have every copper in London looking for it when it's gone. You see, this broach is highly unusual and, well, if you're found trying to sell it—"

"Fine, then! You think of a good way to hand it over. And don't you try and give me the slip. I know where to find you."

"Come to me in three days. I should have a plan by then."

"Aye, you better."

"But don't meet me near the hospital. It's too risky that I'll run into someone I know. Perhaps we've been seen already." Eliza turned and looked up the alley. No one was in sight.

"Where then?" Catherine said.

Eliza turned back. "Someplace farther away, but still busy," she mumbled while thinking hard and fast for a plan.

"Mitre Square, about the same time as now."

"Don't try and cross me."

As Eliza's idea was coming to a realization, she felt herself mentally getting stronger. Then she became angry. "I won't. And don't ever threaten me again." She pointed her finger down at the Catherine's face.

The woman rose slightly, opened her mouth and put it around Eliza's gloved finger, then sucked it. Eliza pulled her hand away, repulsed by the harlot's vile actions. Catherine cackled as Eliza ran.

She heard coins jingling in the pouch from the alleyway behind her.

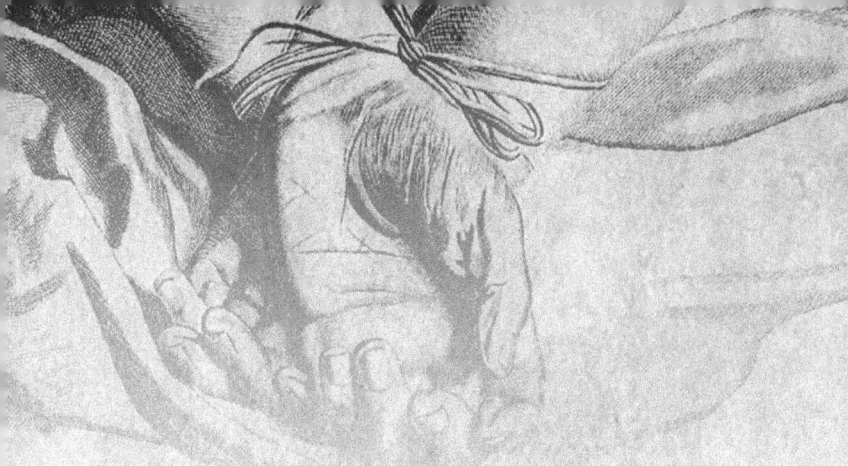

CHAPTER 11

liza barged through the doors of London Hospital out of breath and asking for Doctor Riley. When James met her in the lobby, she pulled him to a corner away from prying eyes. "James, I was robbed."

"What? Here, just outside?" He began to move toward the door. Eliza grabbed his arm and yanked him back. "You can't make a fuss, James. I'm not supposed to be here.

"It's not right. We should send for the police."

"Absolutely not!"

Several people on the other side of the lobby, including the receptionist and two nurses, looked over at them.

"You're being ridiculous," he said. "You could've been hurt."

"But I wasn't. Please understand, James. My father—"

"Yes, don't remind me. I know his temperament all too well."

"Then help."

"How?"

"Have your carriage bring me home."

James stood there for a moment and appeared to be deep in thought. "I'll agree, with one condition."

"What is it? Anything."

"Promise you'll come back and work with me like you did today." He pulled Eliza closer to him and looked into her eyes.

Eliza turned her head and saw the other women in the lobby had continued to stare. "James, I—"

"It was one of the best days I've had in quite some time. Please, I'm not asking for anything else but for us to work together a few times more."

"All right. I'll try."

"Thank you." He lifted her hand and kissed it. "I'll send for the carriage." James gently released her hand, then walked over to the receptionist and nurses standing across the room. A moment later, the receptionist got up from her desk and walked down a long hallway and the nurses dispersed.

While the carriage horses clopped through the East End, Eliza took off her gloves, then reached up and caressed her great grandmother's broach. There wasn't any conceivable way she could give it to a wretch such as Catherine. The mere thought made her seethe and grind her teeth. A moment later, she felt pain and moved her hand away. Eliza had been clutching the broach so hard some of the sharper edges of the setting left minute pinpricks of blood on her palm. She put her hand up and licked the wounds, then put the gloves back on.

The carriage arrived on Queen Anne Street and the driver helped Eliza step out. She thanked him and then headed into the house. Nanette was in the foyer ready to take her hat, coat, and gloves. "Where is Mrs. Sutton?" she said.

"Last I saw, she was bringing your father tea in his study."

"My father's home?"

"Yes, Miss."

"For how long?"

"Since a bit after noon."

"He never comes home early. Is something wrong? What happened?"

"I don't know, Miss."

"Suppose I'll have to go and find out myself. Thank you, Nanette."

The maid curtsied and quickly left the room before Eliza could ask her anymore questions. Eliza slowly walked toward her father's study. She looked into the parlor on the way, hoping her mother would be there to distract her for a while. The room was empty. Knots in her stomach, she stood in front of the study doors gathering her thoughts before knocking.

"Come in, Eliza," her father said.

She turned the crystal knob, which stung her injured palm, and entered the room. Lord Covington sat in a chair next to the fireplace with a book on his lap.

"Hello, Father."

"Come in and close the door. Take a seat next to me here by the fire. You must be chilled. I saw you arrive in an open carriage."

Eliza walked over and sat in the chair opposite his, on the other side of the fireplace. "It's been a long day," she said.

"Was that Doctor Riley's carriage?"

"Yes, it was. I was on my way home and he saw me in Regent's Park. We spoke for a bit and he offered me a ride."

"Why didn't he come with you? I saw no one else in the carriage."

"He was waiting for someone."

"I see. And how is he? Gotten over you by now, I'd think."

"Yes, Father, I'm sure. We are only friends."

"Good. Good."

"What are you reading?" she said, pointing to the book in his lap, changing the subject.

"I was looking through this old picture book your mother kept." Eliza got up and sat on the floor next to her father's chair.

Together they went over the photos and Lord Covington explained each one. What the event was, where it was taken, and all the details. She watched her father's facial expressions go from joy at the earlier pages to somber toward the end when he got to a photo of his grandmother. Eliza treasured these dear moments spent with him; they melted her heart. Until she noticed the diamond broach her grandmother wore pinned to her dress.

That moment turned her heart to stone.

At dinner, Eliza ate very little and her mother took notice.

"If you don't eat, you will get too thin and your dress will have to be altered."

"Let her be, dear. She's had a long day," her father said.

Her mother sighed.

EAST END GIRLS

For the remainder of the courses, Eliza moved food with her silverware back and forth across the china without ever taking a bite. Her thoughts were miles away, but not filled with marriage plans, her wedding night, moving to another country, or regrets about James like her parents might have believed. Eliza felt an intense gnawing in her belly from the inside out over what to do about Catherine.

After dinner, she joined her father in his study hoping to discuss medicine and take her mind off of the predicament she was in.

"You seem bothered, Eliza. Pour yourself a bit of brandy and come sit by the fire."

"I'm all right, Father. Professor Huxley announced the graduates today."

"Ah, and it's all coming down on you like a ton of bricks now is it?"

"I suppose."

Eliza changed her mind and poured herself a bit of brandy, brought her father a snifter full and then sat down with hers, taking small sips while her father talked about his day.

"Mother said you were called in early today. Is everything all right with the Royals?"

"Yes, fine. One of the visiting little grand princes got a bit of the sniffles is all."

"Oh."

"We haven't spoken much about you going off to America. I imagine this must be weighing heavy on your thoughts, but you shouldn't worry. Henry's a smart man. He won't leave you alone in a strange place."

"He'll be busy working late nights, I imagine."

"What will you do?"

"Bring my graduation papers, find work if I can. Volunteer at hospitals if I have to."

"Do you think Henry would allow it?"

"If he doesn't want me to go mad he will."

Lord Covington laughed, then took a swig of brandy and swallowed. He said nothing.

"You don't think he'll want me to practice?" she said.

"I don't know. We haven't spoken about it."

"If you do, can you mention it to him? Persuade him, perhaps?"

"I'll try," he said, then took another drink.

Eliza wasn't comforted by their conversations this evening like she usually was. The talk only made her more nervous and upset about the future.

When she went to bed that night, she thought further on how to remedy the situation with Catherine. Dreams of hate and murder kept her mind occupied.

CHAPTER 12

rs. Sutton, would you please send a note to Ann Williams this morning? Ask her if it would be all right if I call on her this afternoon."

"Yes, Miss."

"Well," her mother said. "It's about time. I'd almost forgotten myself."

"Do you think she'll see me on such short notice?"

"She hardly ever leaves the house these days. I'm sure she'll be happy for your visit, but why the sudden interest?"

"It's been too long, and I may not get another chance. Exams are next month, then graduation, then the wedding, and then I leave."

"Don't make it all sound so rushed."

"But it is."

"Oh Eliza, you have such a talent for dramatics."

"I do not."

Eliza's father entered the room. "It's too early for

bickering, ladies." He took a seat at the breakfast table. "If you continue, I'll leave without taking a single bite."

Eliza and her mother both leaned back in their chairs and finished eating their toast.

"I say, now that's more like it," he said.

During classes, Eliza debated whether to go and work with James as she'd promised. Then it came to her that it would probably be best if she went when it was time to meet Catherine again. The vivid dreams and nightmares she'd had the past couple nights— in bits and pieces—had given her an idea. A plan she knew would work if done exactly right. She just needed time and a clear mind to devise it and see it through.

More than ever, she looked forward to visiting with Ann Williams later that afternoon. Eliza hoped she might improve her friend's melancholy situation and forget about her own tumultuous one. At least for Eliza's sake, she was sure Ann would leave her house to attend the wedding in December. Eliza hated to see any acquaintance of hers upset or sad.

On her way home, she stopped at White's Chocolate House on St. James Street and had a cup to drink, then picked up several pieces of eating chocolate for Ann. For the first time in days, she didn't feel the presence of anyone watching her. She was certain then that it was Catherine who had been following her the entire time. There was no detective, no one her father had hired. Eliza was fortunate the woman never approached her in public. It was also good she hadn't got hurt. Catherine could have attacked her and simply stolen the broach. These thoughts made Eliza's heart beat harder and faster. She clenched her hands into fists. A slow building heat full of rage moved from her chest upward, coating the skin around her neck and head with fire. Eliza, who was certain her face must be brick red, took in deep breaths to try to calm herself before arriving home earlier than usual. She didn't need any unwanted attention from her mother.

There was no one in the foyer when she came through the front doors, so she ran upstairs and began to change into something more appropriate for her visit with Ann. After she was dressed, Nanette came in and helped her fix her hair.

"Did Mrs. Sutton say that Mrs. Williams would see me? We could be doing this all for nothing."

"She did, Miss. The carriage is waiting for you out front."

"Thank you."

"You're welcome, and don't forget the little box of eating chocolates I saw on the foyer table. If Lord Covington or your mother sees them they might very well disappear."

Eliza laughed. "Funny how they say they dislike it, but behind closed doors…"

Nanette smiled. "I'll meet you downstairs to help you with your coat and hat." Then she left the room.

Moments later, Eliza was out the door and in the carriage to go just up the street. Any other day she would have walked, but it was drizzling out, and she wanted to look her best for Ann, whom she hadn't seen in quite some time.

When she arrived at the William's home, she was greeted at the front door by one of the maids, then brought to Ann who had been waiting for her in the atrium with a tray of tea and cookies on a side table. The William's house was lovely and Eliza had always thought it suited them.

Doctor Jonathan Williams was recently knighted by the Queen and worked sometimes alongside Eliza's father on more difficult cases. Ann had married him when she was 22. He was ten years her senior and it was a bit of a scandal because of his rank in society at the time, but then it was all soon gotten over because of his excellent skill and reputation.

Since then, Ann had gone into a deep depression because her father's tin business went under and as hard as she and Jon tried, she was unable to get pregnant. All the solemn news was too much for Eliza to handle with everything she had going on in her own life. She tried her best to comfort Ann and divert her attention when she could, but all Ann's woes, along with being unable to get pregnant, kept Eliza away. But she had the excuse of medical school and her own wedding to plan. Ann of all people knew the amount of work and education involved with becoming a physician.

When Eliza entered the room Ann looked up and stood to greet her. "You look absolutely radiant," Ann said in a monotone voice. Her face was peaked and expressionless.

Eliza smiled. She had hoped her attire and attitude would bring some cheer to her friend, but it didn't seem to have worked. Despite her kind welcome, there was deep hurt and longing in Ann's eyes. "Forgive me for not coming to see you sooner. How have you been?" Eliza said.

The two women hugged. "Please, sit down," Ann said, pointing to the spot on the settee next to where she had been seated a moment ago.

Feeling the weight of the day's classes, and work, along with the sad expression on her friend's face, Eliza sank into the cushion when she sat. The Williams's maid began pouring them cups of tea. "Just a bit of milk in mine, please," Eliza said.

After the servant left, Eliza reached for Ann's hands and turned to face her. "Please, my dear friend. Tell me how you truly are and don't hold back."

Ann's eyes immediately filled with tears. Before Eliza could pull a handkerchief from her sleeve, her friend was crying. Eliza handed it to Ann, and she dabbed her eyes. "I'm sorry, it's just that things have been…well, they've been horrible."

"Please, tell me. What is it?" Eliza said. "Is it Sir Jon?" Ann nodded.

"Has he done something against you?"

She nodded again.

"This is horrible news indeed," Eliza said. "Another woman?" Her friend nodded again.

So, the rumors are true. Doctor Williams practiced at the London Hospital in East End. He performed abortions on prostitutes as well, but overcharged for them, which was not honorable in Eliza's eyes. She'd also heard stories that he might've been having affairs with some of these women. It disgusted her. She could feel hatred rising from the pit of her stomach.

Ann slowed her crying to whimpering. Eliza offered her the cup of tea the maid had just poured. She raised the cup and saucer and took a small sip. "Thank you," she said.

"Don't think of it," Eliza said. "Thanking me, I mean."

"I can do nothing but, and not about thanking you, but about *her*."

"Do you have a name? Is it someone you know?"

Ann shook her head, and then after a whimper, she said, "Mary Kelly."

"I've not heard the name before."

"She might be a prostitute." Ann started crying again and Eliza took the teacup from her shaking hand and set it down on the table. Then she held her friend while Ann cried for at least ten minutes more.

"I will never quite understand how you endure it," Eliza said.

"Maybe after you're married it will come to light."

"I hope not. I'd like to leave some of *the ways* of English marriage behind when we go."

"That's a shocking thing to say."

"And what you've told me isn't? It pains me to see you like this."

Ann wiped her face one last time with Eliza's handkerchief, then handed it back to her. There were very few signs on her face that showed she had just been crying. She looked almost the way she did when Eliza first walked into the room. It was simultaneously sad and amazing to see her friend so changeable. Eliza worried that Ann might be skirting the edge of mental illness, possibly mania, and she wanted to help her friend before it was too late. Time was running out, though. She would be leaving very early the next year. Eliza wondered what she could do.

EAST END GIRLS

It was all the fault of the East End harlots. Eliza's hate for them had been gradually worsening, and this last bit of news had brought it to its peak. The prostitutes used to be a means of learning the worst cases of venereal disease and the female anatomy, but now they'd become a nuisance. Eliza thought about how it could be that these women's lives could be so intertwined with women like her and Ann Williams. It just didn't seem possible. Times were changing, and she could already feel its effect on her.

And she didn't like it.

It had been three long days since Catherine threatened Eliza with a scheme of blackmail. Three days during which Eliza's loathing for the whores of the East End continued to grow.

She worked alongside Doctor James Riley, but he couldn't have enjoyed it the same way he did before, since Eliza was now always so distant and deep in thought about meeting up with Catherine and her visit the other day with her friend, Ann Williams. James tried several times to be humorous, or strike up a conversation, and failed miserably at getting her attention. It wasn't until he asked how she and Henry were getting along that she woke from her daze.

"What?" Eliza whispered.

"Have you heard a word I've said? What has your mind so occupied these days?"

"I'm sorry, James. It's the exams, the wedding, moving. Tell me something, do you know Sir Jon Williams very well?"

"I wouldn't say I know him *very* well, but I see him on occasion here and we talk about medicine. Why?"

"Have you heard any rumors about him?"

"These halls are filled with talk about other people, but I don't bother paying attention to any of it and neither should you."

"Do you think it's true he sees prostitutes?"

"Well, of course he sees them. Sir Jon is here every Friday to perform abortions."

"That's not what I mean, and I think it's wrong of him to make them pay so much."

"He accepts what they can afford. It's better than having one done on the street."

"You don't understand what I'm trying to say."

"And what exactly is it? You think Sir Jon is having an affair with a prostitute? Don't be silly. You need to get that notion out of your head. Talk like that can ruin your career. And his. Let's take a break and have some tea. Then we can discuss what it really is you're trying to say."

"I'll be fine."

"I know I made you promise to work with me a few more times, but I understand you're busy, and if you'd rather not—"

"James, I'm all right. A promise is a promise. Let's just finish up the day and go home."

Doctor Riley lowered his head. "My intention was for us to enjoy the last few times we would see one another doing something we both love, not for you to be in a rush and leave."

"Forgive me. Truly, I'm in no hurry to go. I never was. Please believe me when I tell you that I want to spend these moments with you. The memories I'll take with me and cherish always."

Eliza saw James's eyes well up. He turned away and spoke. "Don't apologize. It was my own selfishness that wanted this and if it hurts me, then only I'm to blame."

She took him by the arm. "I think I'd like some tea now," she said, and then she led him down the hall with a broken heart and a mind seething with rage.

Eliza left the London Hospital in the rain and told the driver to circle around before heading to Mitre Square. He did, and it gave her a little more time to ready herself. She put on her black cloak and pulled the hood over. There was a small pouch of money underneath where she kept the leather case of instruments. Eliza pulled it out and pushed it down into the pocket of her coat.

The driver stopped and pounded on the roof of the cab. Eliza stepped out, paid the man, and started walking in the rain. It wasn't long before she felt someone following her. *I know this game, and I can play, too.* She ducked down an alley, picked up her pace, and made a few quick turns, then stopped. Twenty feet in front of her, stood Catherine, looking side to side down backstreets in a frantic search.

"Lose something?" Eliza said.

Catherine swung around and gasped. "There you are, Miss. Thought you might be trying to give me the slip." She went over to where Eliza was standing.

"I would never do something like that."

"I knew you were a smart girl. Now, tell me your plan."

"Remember I told you if the broach went missing, the police would go looking for it?"

"I do."

"Well, I've found a jeweler who will disassemble it for me so that I can give you the loose diamonds to sell individually. They'll be unable to trace it that way."

"Shame to break up such a pretty piece."

"Do you want the deal or not? It's the best I can do."

"How long will it take?"

"By Michaelmas."

"That long?"

"It's only two weeks, and besides, it's a delicate matter."

"I suppose it'll make for a great holiday surprise. For me anyhow." She cackled and then started coughing. Cleared her throat, then spat to the right. "What am I supposed to do in the meantime? I need a little drink now and then. Helps me keep my mouth shut if you know what I mean."

Eliza shoved her hand down into the cloak pocket and pulled out the pouch. "Here's five schillings. Should keep you quiet for a while."

"Indeed, Miss. It will." Catherine smiled, exposing her missing tooth and grungy mouth.

"Meet me back here Michaelmas night."

"Good idea. Lots of people will be out celebrating, me right along with them."

"I don't want to see you until then, and if I feel you following me, the deal's off."

"No need to make threats. I'll leave ya be."

Catherine walked away shaking the coin pouch, humming a song Eliza didn't recognize, which didn't surprise her. She wanted nothing in common with this vile and loathsome woman.

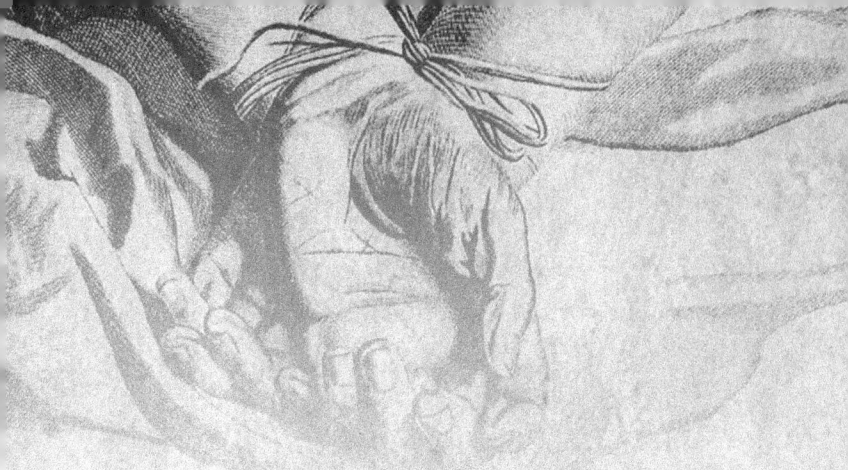

CHAPTER 13

September 29th, the Covington house was filled with happy familiar faces ready for Michaelmas cheer. For Eliza, though, the holiday no longer seemed a joyous occasion as she often found herself checking the time. Doctor Llewellyn had come for dinner and Eliza's father was very happy to see his old friend again, but it meant she would have less time to spend with him. The men would finish their meals, then be drinking and smoking cigars until it was time to retire. Lady Covington would excuse herself and go to bed early blaming an exhaustion headache for all the work she did to make the dinner party a success.

"Eliza, there you are, darling. I've missed you." Henry stepped up, leaned in and gave her a simple kiss on the cheek. There was no passion in it. She felt domestic already and wondered whom he was truly saving his desires for.

"It's good to see you again," she said.

"I'm looking forward to when I see you every day."

She smiled. *I'm sure of it.* "I think it's time to sit down for dinner. We should go before my mother sends someone to look for us."

"I hope she placed us close to one another. Sometimes I'm certain your parents are determined to keep us apart until the wedding." He put his arm around her and pulled her close. Eliza moved out of his embrace. "What's wrong?"

"Nothing. Now come on." She took his hand and led him away.

The dining room was elegant. There were twenty chairs lining either side of the long rectangular king's table. Candlelight flickered off the silverware and set aglow the white and yellow rose bouquets. It appeared as though Mr. Grey and all his botanical knowledge had come through. No doubt, he'd be doing the flower arrangements for the wedding.

"There you are. Henry, you're over here next to me," Lady Covington said. He turned to Eliza and winked before walking to his seat. "Eliza, you're next to Doctor Llewellyn." Her mother pointed to the other end of the table.

Eliza grinned and hurried over. The doctor rose and pulled out her chair. "I'm delighted you were able to join us," she said.

"It was generous of your family to have invited me."

"Is your wife here? I'd very much like to meet her." Eliza looked up and down the table.

"She passed away two years ago."

"Oh, I'm so sorry." *I might've known that if Father had kept up your friendship.*

"Please, don't be. She's in a better place."

"Yes," was all Eliza could say. Doctor Llewellyn took a drink of wine and she did the same.

In perfect time, Mr. Sutton brought out a platter with a cooked goose on top. He set it down in front of them. Eliza eyed its spread legs, stuffing spilling from the cavity. In her mind she saw Annie Chapman and thought of how she'd pulled out her intestines, piling them over to one side so they would be out of the way. Immediately, her appetite disappeared.

"Any news?" she said.

Doctor Llewellyn looked at her and wrinkled his brow.

"Concerning Whitechapel."

"Just conjecture. No solid leads. I even heard Inspector Abberline came by for a visit with a midwife theory."

"That he did, but I'm sure I redirected him."

"So, you don't think it's possible the killer is a woman?"

Eliza struggled to come up with a response, but then Llewellyn spared her by putting his hand over hers. "I'm in agreement with you." He gently turned her hand palm side up. "No one would think these hands could be used for anything but good." The tiny scabs from where the broach had pricked her were still barely visible, but Doctor Llewellyn made no mention of them.

Lord Covington, seated at the very end of the table, raised his glass and tapped it with a spoon. Eliza slid her hand out of Doctor Llewellyn's. There was something she didn't like about his touch, and now she wished she were sitting next to Henry after all. Her father cleared his throat and made a longwinded holiday toast to his friends and family. He mentioned her upcoming graduation, wedding, and even choked up a bit when he spoke of her leaving for America. There were a few yawns during the speech and more than one couple was distracted whispering to one another, so that when he finally got to the end of it, everyone cheered, and Eliza knew it wasn't because she was moving after the wedding, but she couldn't help feel that way.

An hour before midnight Eliza sneaked out of the house. The air outside was thick with a cold damp fog. Benches normally visible in the daylight hours had completely vanished. The dense haze made the surrounding gas lamps ineffective. They reminded her of the way a lighthouse appeared from a ship's point of view, dim and feeble.

A few more people were out than usual at the late hour and she assumed it was because of the holiday. Their footsteps tapped on the wet cobblestones, the sounds coming from all directions before anyone would actually physically appear. They walked through the fog and it moved around them like a ghostly smoke dragon. She considered returning home more than once, crawling into her warm bed, and ignoring Catherine's demands. Who did this prostitute think she was that she could blackmail anybody? It angered Eliza to be caught in the middle of such a vile woman's scheme. She shouldn't have to sneak around in bad weather. Her nose was bitter cold, and watery mucous ran from her nostrils, over her lips, leaving a salty taste in her mouth. She wiped it away with her sleeve. Eliza feared the possibility she might become ill and be unable to finish her final exams. These thoughts only fueled her rage as she rushed through Regent's Park wearing a frock coat and hooded cloak, the doctor's bag clutched in her hand.

Eliza followed the louder sounds of hooves clopping; it wasn't long before she was able to get a hansom cab. While inside, she opened her bag and rearranged it, putting the items she'd need on top. The carriage came to a halt and the driver knocked on the roof. Eliza stepped out into a large puddle of murky water, sending up the odor of raw sewage. She clenched her jaw and ground her teeth together, then covered her nose with a scarf she'd stolen from Nanette and paid the man. He pulled away to avoid splashing her, and she was thankful for it.

When he was out of sight, Eliza went toward Mitre Square. There were even more people out on the streets at East End than usual. She knew Catherine would be one of them. Every few minutes, someone would come out of the fog and if it weren't for the all the wine she'd had at dinner, she'd probably be a little jumpy.

A block away from the square, she heard a woman shouting slurred obscenities. Eliza walked softly behind where the sounds were coming from. She looked down an alley and saw the shadow figure of Catherine leaning against one of the walls. As Eliza approached, a small group of loud partygoers were walking by. She set her medical bag down and then crept closer, her footfalls silent compared to all the noise. Catherine was drunk and shouting at them about how she would soon be rich.

Eliza's heart sped up as she quietly waited behind the prostitute. After the people had passed, the prostitute took in a deep breath and paused. As she exhaled, Eliza held up the ends of Nanette's scarf, which were tightly wound around each of her hands, leaving some space left in between. Eliza quickly brought the scarf down hard against the prostitute's throat. Catherine tried to scream, but her words were choked off by the pressure against her neck. Eliza dragged the kicking, thrashing woman into the alley. The backward movement and struggle only made the scarf tighten more, and Catherine's choking turned to weak gasps for air. After about fifteen feet, the prostitute's fight slowed. The fog hid them in the alley. Eliza could no longer see the street at the other end. She continued to pull Catherine by the scarf until the woman's body went limp. When it did, Eliza moved the fabric away and let her body fall to the ground. She came around and kneeled beside the body, took her right glove off and checked for a pulse. The prostitute was still alive, barely, which was what Eliza had wanted. She put her glove back on, and then reached into the medical bag she had placed there earlier. The surgical knife was right on top.

Nanette's scarf had left deep red marks across Catherine's throat. While positioning herself over the unconscious harlot, Eliza lifted up her own skirts, forgetting that they'd been splashed with sewage. When she caught a whiff of the foul stench that soaked the hems, that made her even more furious, so she plopped herself down hard onto Catherine's abdomen. The woman groaned underneath her. Eliza leaned forward and stared at the wretched woman's face. Hate filled her with an extreme heat that spread throughout her extremities. Eliza tightened her grip around the knife and gritted her teeth. Catherine opened her eyes and saw Eliza on top of her. With one long stroke of her arm she sliced through Catherine's neck. The prostitute convulsed between Eliza's legs. She moved her lips and tried to talk, but no words could escape. There was only a gurgling sound that came from the open wound as hot blood pulsed out, steam rising from its crimson flows.

Still enraged, Eliza slashed the long, drawn face she hated more than anything in the world. *One V for vile, and one for vulgar!* The carving didn't stop until Catherine's body ceased to twitch. Eliza envisioned the woman's pupils dilating. She wanted to see the woman die and be the last person the whore saw before she did. Eliza exhaled a deep sigh of relief. The torment of being blackmailed was over. It was time to cover up her crime and make it the Whitechapel Murderer's. She got off the body and kneeled down next to it. Eliza pulled up Catherine's skirts and began her work below. She took her time, remembering how she'd cut up Annie Chapman. It had to look the same, but progressively worse. In honor of Professor Huxley humiliating her because she'd confused the kidneys with the ovaries, she excised one for him, as well as the uterus. Eliza thought of what her father had said that night in his study. *"The killer is evolving."*

"Indeed, father," she whispered. "The killer most certainly is." She finished laying the extracted uterus and kidney onto Nanette's scarf. Eliza was tying up the ends when she heard a police whistle and shouting somewhere in the fog. Uncertain of the direction or distance of the sounds, she hurried the rest of what she was doing. Out of fabric to clean her instruments, she cut off half of Catherine's apron. Small bits of junk came out of the pockets and landed scattered on and around the body. Eliza shoved the cloth into her pocket, then set the organs in her medical bag, and stood up. She pulled the cloak hood over her head and walked quickly into the boggy mist, avoiding any people out on the streets.

After passing a man who nearly bumped into her, then pardoned himself, Eliza ducked into a dark doorway, took the swatch of cloth from her pocket, and quickly wiped off her dirty instruments. She threw the fabric down, placed her tools back into the medical bag and continued walking. Then another police whistle blew. This one seemed much louder. She picked up the pace, her heart racing and pounding in her chest. She rounded a corner and a horse reared up and neighed. Eliza shrieked and jumped to the left. The animal came down, hooves clapping like thunder against the cobblestone. A carriage door swung open with a shadow of a man in its opening. His gloved hand reached out to Eliza.

"Get in, quick."

She took hold and climbed in.

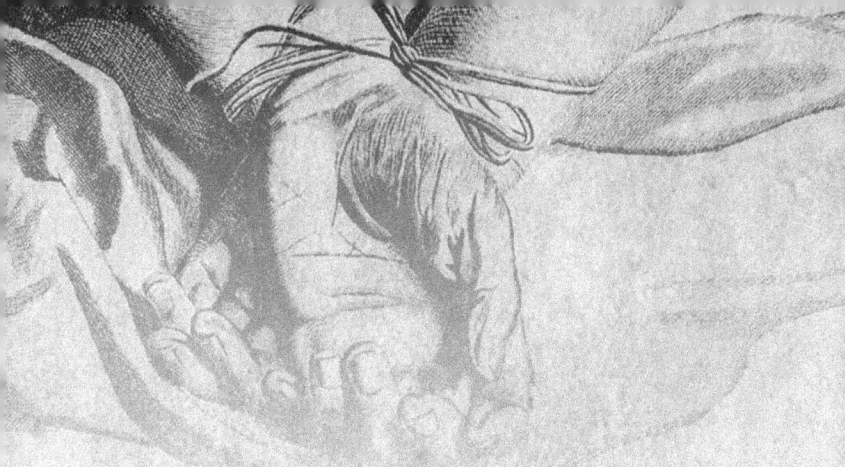

CHAPTER 14

liza sat down in the seat across from the man. Their black leather gloves stuck together for a moment before pulling apart. "Thank you, Sir," she said.

He tipped the rim of his top hat forward, which hid his face even more. The only distinguishable feature was his pointy chin. Everything else was veiled in shadows. Eliza examined his attire. It appeared he was a gentleman of some sort based on his fashionable suit. As her stare moved over his clothes, she could feel him watching her in return.

"Where shall I tell my man to take you?" His voice was low and deep.

"Regent's Park, please Sir."

He tapped the roof of the carriage with a cane Eliza hadn't noticed before. The handle was made of bronze formed into the shape of a serpent's head. Red rubies were inlaid for the eyes. It was quite elegant.

Eliza sat back and put her hands together in her lap. The gloves stuck to one another. Pulling them apart filled the coach with a muted sound of tearing paper and she wondered why blood had to be such a tacky substance. *Had the gentleman noticed when he took her hand? Then again his glove seemed sticky, too.*

The carriage rode on, and Eliza sat with a small smile on her face and eyed the carriage's interior as an excuse to observe more details about the gentleman. The legs of his pants were as wet as the bottom of her hem. She could make nothing else out about him since he wore nothing but black. If someone was to look upon the pair, they'd think they were either going to, or coming from, a funeral. Then something next to the man's feet caught Eliza's eye. It stopped her breath. A medical bag very much like hers was on the floor of the carriage to his right. A feeling of panic sped up her heart rate. She looked at him and she could tell his eyes were already on her face.

"It is late for a woman of Regent's Park to be out in such a dangerous part of the city," he said.

Eliza took a deep breath to calm herself. "I was visiting friends."

An odor clung to the air between them—the smell of metal and salt—a scent of blood. It couldn't all be emanating from her. She moved forward, closer to the man, then inhaled deeply. The man sat up and grabbed her wrist. "What is it, Miss? Are you faint?"

"No, sir."

He let go of her and this time, it was *his* glove that stuck to hers. They eyed one another. Heart muscles tightened within her chest.

The carriage stopped, and a moment later, the door opened. "Regent's Park," the driver said. Eliza took her medical bag and stepped down.

She turned around and looked up at the man in the carriage. "Who shall I thank, sir?"

The gentleman tipped his hat forward again and smiled, bringing together thin slivers of pink flesh above the pointy chin. "Simply a good Samaritan, Miss."

"Thank you, then."

"Remember not to travel at the East End late at night. For your own safety."

"Yes, sir."

The driver shut the door and Eliza walked into the park as fast as she could. The carriage pulled away, and when the sounds were barely audible, Eliza headed home. For a moment, she wondered if he would have his driver follow her, but then she came to her senses and was sure paranoia must be setting in.

Once more, Eliza came quietly through the servants' entrance. Then she unfastened her skirts and let them drop to the floor. She rinsed the hems, her cape, and coat with her gloves on, then left everything hanging over a chair for Nanette to wash better the next day. In the kitchen, she opened her medical bag on the cutting block table, took out the wrapped organs, then walked over and placed them on the hearth fire. She listened to them sizzle and crackle for a while, entranced by the orange and yellow flames licking and devouring the pieces of a whore. Before leaving, she added a few more logs and stoked the fire to keep it hot and burning high.

Eliza went upstairs to her room and fell asleep thinking of the good Samaritan.

And wondering whether or not he was truly all that good.

The next morning, Eliza and her parents arrived home from church and were told by Mr. Sutton that several men were waiting to speak with Lord Covington in his study. After her father went to greet them, Eliza joined her mother in the parlor for tea.

"Why are there so many people here? And who are they?" Lady Covington said.

"Mr. Sutton told me that there's an Inspector Abberline, an Inspector Dew, and a Detective Halse here. Along with two police surgeons, Doctors Sequeira and Brown," Mrs. Sutton said.

"Something more must have happened in Whitechapel. What else do you know?"

"Papers say there were two women murdered last night. *London Star's* calling him Jack the Ripper now. He wrote a letter taunting the police and everything."

"Two?" Eliza said. Her mind went straight to the gentleman in the carriage. The smell inside, how their gloves kept sticking, and his medical bag on the floor. Could he have been The Whitechapel Murderer? This Jack the Ripper? Her mother's voice pulled her away from the idea.

EAST END GIRLS

"The world has gone mad, Mrs. Sutton. From now on Eliza, you're to use one of our carriages to get to and from the university. Don't even think of refusing me."

Eliza didn't argue. There was no point in it, and she needed to take the advice of the gentleman Samaritan and stay away from the East End. Only if it was necessary to brush up on the female anatomy to pass her exams would she give it another go; otherwise she'd stay away.

Nearly two hours had passed when her father finally came into the parlor. He told Mrs. Sutton they would need to dine early.

"What on earth for?" her mother said.

"The men would like me to join them later at the station." "The police station?"

"Well, I can't very well have them at the gentlemen's club now can I?"

"Indeed, you cannot."

Then Eliza wondered if her Samaritan went to clubs. He was certainly dressed for it. Her father turned his attention to her. "Seems I was right, and the murderer has become more vicious. This is why they need my insight."

Her mother turned toward the two talking and listened.

"You must help them, Father. I just wish there was something I could do, too."

"Thomas," said her mother. "I've told your daughter she's not to leave this house without taking one of our carriages. I won't have it."

"Yes, dear," he said. "I'm sure Eliza is well aware of the situation." He looked at his daughter and rolled his eyes.

Eliza smiled and took a sip of tea.

For the next week, the family's carriage took Eliza everywhere she needed to go. She didn't want to admit it, but riding in the coach with the curtains closed really did make her feel safe. Even though she knew Catherine Eddowes—the *London Star* had revealed the prostitute's surname—was no longer following her, Eliza wondered if her gentlemen Samaritan friend might come looking around. She thought he could have the same curiosities about her that she had for him. And what would he think about her evolving his brutality without his own hand in it? Perhaps he'd be angry with her for bringing so much attention to himself. Maybe he was plotting to kill her, or even worse, expose the truth. The thoughts would drive her mad if she continued this way.

The Samaritan was a gentleman and therefore would be educated. He wouldn't allow himself to be caught under any circumstances. Besides, he'd been killing prostitutes and women of ill-repute in the East End. It was obvious he knew Eliza didn't belong there, had even said as much. She had nothing to worry about. Soon enough she'd be a graduate physician and then married off. Her heart sunk as the last of her thoughts seemed rather dull. What would living with Henry be like compared to saving lives and taking them, blackmail, and riding in a carriage with Jack the Ripper? She knew exactly what it would be like—it would be suffocating.

After breakfast, Nanette, who'd smartly kept quiet about having to wash the filthy skirts, cloak, and frock coat, helped Eliza put on a different coat, hat, and gloves. Then, while Eliza waited for the family carriage to pull up front, an altogether different one raced from up the street and halted at the gate in a peculiar angle. Eliza couldn't help but think it might be Jack the Ripper, her Samaritan gentleman, come to call—or kill. Her heart began to race. The carriage's driver came round and opened the door. To Eliza's surprise, a servant stepped down and was hurriedly walking toward the house. Eliza went out and met the woman at the gate, just as her own carriage pulled up. It was the Williams's maid, her eyes teary and full of fear. "Please, Miss," the maid said. "It's Mrs. Williams. She needs you as fast as you can come."

Eliza told her driver she'd be riding in the Williams's carriage. He nodded and turned around. Then she followed the Williams's maid into their carriage. "What happened?" Eliza said. The carriage sped up the street, bouncing them around in the back.

"Sir Jon left early. You know he spends Fridays helping the poor at London Hospital."

"Yes, yes, I know." *Although we're both well aware he's doing more than that.*

"I went to help Mrs. Williams dress for breakfast and found her still in bed. She wasn't coming to. I even shook her."

"But why send for me? Doctor Williams is—"

"This fell from her hand." The maid passed a small glass bottle to Eliza. She raised it and took a whiff. The scent was mildly astringent. A label on the outside of the bottle read, *laudanum*. "There was another empty one on her night table next to the bed."

Eliza's heart sank. Laudanum was useful in small doses, but deadly in large amounts. She was about to yell out at the driver to hurry when the carriage pulled up to the Williams's house. The two women opened the door and climbed out on their own, then ran into the house. Ann's body was as the maid had described it, sprawled out across the bed. She was alive, but her breathing was very slow and her pulse faint. "Does anyone else know?" Eliza said.

"No," the maid said. "Not even the driver. I shut the door when I left and told the rest of them to stay out. That Mrs. Williams was feeling ill today."

"Good. Then it would make sense that you called for me—very smart. "What's your name?"

"It's Abigail, Miss."

"All right, Abigail, let's get Mrs. Williams sitting up in bed. We'll need to wash her, change the clothes she has on. Have someone in the kitchen make her some tea. Tell them to knock first, and then you take the tray. I'll also need you to send your driver to the Royal Free Hospital to tell a Professor Huxley I will not be attending classes today."

"Yes, Miss."

"Let's use cool water."

Eliza helped Abigail with every aspect of the care. Ann urinated on herself and soaked the bed sheets only an hour after they'd got her dressed, so they had to go through the entire routine again, but all the commotion seemed to be causing her to stir. Off and on she'd been opening her eyes. Eliza held a candle near Ann's face to get a better look and noted that her pupils were pinpoints.

The maid gently held her head, while Ann took several sips of tea. After which she lay back against the pillows, then suddenly sat straight up with bulging eyes and opened her mouth. A dark liquid shot across the bed in a steady stream. Eliza and Abigail looked at one another with wide eyes.

Ann groaned and then lay down again. For the next hour, she would rouse, vomit, and then pass out, but she was becoming much more coherent during the times she was awake. Pushing away the cup of tea and shaking her head no.

It was late afternoon when Eliza thought Ann was stable enough for her to leave. She gave Abigail strict instructions to follow, and she was to send for her again if there were any problems. "When does Sir Jon come home?" Eliza said.

"Not 'til very late on Fridays, Miss."

"Good. Try and keep him away from her if you can, for the next day or so."

"That shouldn't be a problem. They've been sleeping in separate rooms for months. Hardly talk to one another at all anymore."

"Has she done this before?"

Abigail lowered her eyes and nodded. "It was never as bad as this, Miss."

Sweltering rage filled Eliza's chest. She took in a deep breath which only compounded the sensation of hate rising beneath her ribcage. Eliza rushed to the bedroom door, swung it open and headed for the foyer.

"Shall I call for the carriage?" the maid said.

"No, thank you. I'll walk."

Stepping out into the cold air felt like a sledgehammer against her chest so full of heat and rage. Eliza couldn't exhale fast enough and began choking on the Williams's porch. She started walking before anyone saw and came to assist her.

How could Sir Jon be so cruel? Her boot heels clacked against the icy street and the sounds resonated from the high treetops. *Were all men this way? Perhaps even her father?* She didn't want to know or even think it. Men were inherently lecherous, it seemed, and there was no way to prevent it—except to perhaps, eliminate the temptation.

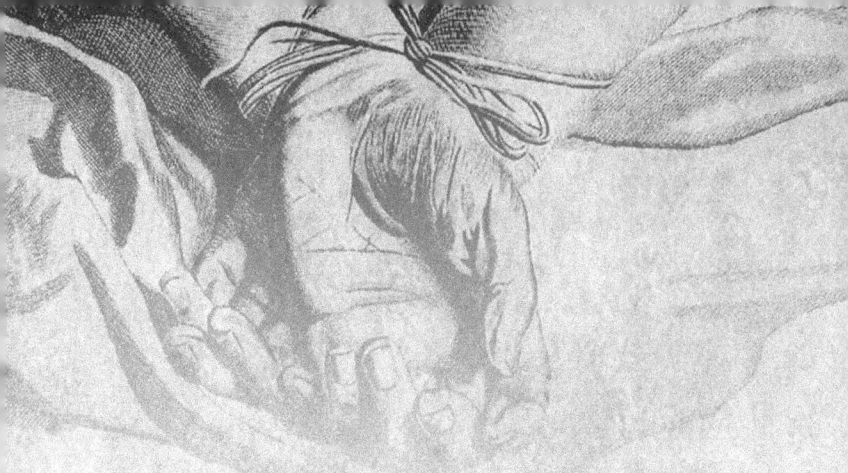

CHAPTER 15

nn Williams had sent a basket of fresh fruit to the Covington household two days later. "My goodness," Eliza's mother said. "How lovely, and grapes, too. Very decadent for this time of year, she must have special ordered them. Apparently, your visit with her went well, although she was a bit late in sending her regards." She picked up a piece of toast and nibbled at a corner.

"We merely caught up on what had been happening in our lives. Ann is a wonderful person and a dear friend, if a bit awkward in society."

"I only wish she would come out more. It would do her a world of good. It's a shame she can't have children. I've heard rumors of Sir Jon's affairs."

"Mother!"

"Well, I won't give you any details, but Ann should be out showing support for him and not mulling around at home. It only lets everyone know the rumors are true. Maybe you should mention it to her on your next visit. I assume you'll be seeing her again."

"Maybe. I'm busy these next few weeks." Eliza finished her tea.

"Which reminds me, the baker—"

"Mother, you choose. Please, for anything else that comes up, pick what you would have wanted for your own wedding. I trust your tastes and know you'll arrange the wedding of the century. My suggestions will only make it drab and I know how important this is to you."

"Eliza, you can't be serious."

"I am."

"But it's *your* special day."

"And it will be even more special if you arrange everything, Mother."

Tears began to swell in her mother's eyes. She raised a napkin to dab them. Eliza rose from her chair, walked over, and kissed her on the cheek. "I've got to head out now, but promise me you'll take care of all the wedding plans."

"Of course, dear, but you should have eaten something more." Eliza left the room before her mother burst into tears. It was apparent she was on the verge. What mother doesn't dream of planning her only daughter's wedding? And be fortunate enough to have one like Eliza who wants no part in it.

Soon there would be obligatory dinners to attend at the Osborne's home and holiday gatherings. Time was running out and then she'd be married and have to move. The life she knew and loved was coming to an end, but she had no intention of giving it up quietly.

No. Not quietly at all.

EAST END GIRLS

The Royal Free Hospital on Henrietta Street, associated with The London School of Medicine for Women, was a teaching hospital. The girls would make their rounds and take notes which Professor Huxley would go over the following day. It was busier than usual, so Eliza and her classmates were spread throughout the building, seeing patients on their own. Vagrants were lined up one after the other, waiting behind makeshift partitions of thin sheets used for curtains.

Eliza walked over to an isolated corner and pulled back the linen. A pretty young woman with blonde hair, not nearly as fair or golden as hers, sat at the edge of a table. She looked up when Eliza rifled through her medical papers. Her eyes were a pale blue compared to Eliza's bright ones. "Hello, Miss. Can you tell me when the doctor will be in to see me?"

"I am the doctor."

"Oh, I'm sorry. I just thought that—"

"I was a nurse."

She smiled and nodded.

Eliza continued flipping through the pages, then went back to the first one and froze. Eyes wide, she looked at the woman and then back down at the notes. "Your name?" she said.

"Mary Kelly, just like it says on those papers you've been reading."

A bit uppity for a prostitute. It was an extremely convenient coincidence however, and had to have more meaning than to simply taunt her. Fate was telling her what she had to do. Thinking quick, she brushed off the harlot's snippy remark. "Sometimes the nurses make mistakes and put the wrong papers in the room. I imagine you'd feel better if I made sure this was really you."

"Oh, yes, Miss, I mean, doctor. I'm sorry, just a bit nervous is all, and I'd like to be heading back to East End before dark."

"I understand. How can I help you?" She hoped it was syphilis. "Well, if I can trust you." Mary spoke with a honeyed voice and looked up with angelic eyes. Eliza could see how this pathetic charm might work on Sir Jon, but she wanted nothing more than to slit this woman's throat right this very moment.

"I assure you. I'm as silent as the grave."

"Well, I suppose. You are a doctor, right?"

"Yes, I am." *Or rather, will be, very soon.*

Mary looked her up and down for a moment, took in a deep breath then spoke softly. "I've been seeing a gentleman as of late, and I mean a *real* gentleman. He's got no children of his own and I'd like to give him one or more."

The rage began to swell within Eliza. Heat erupted from her chest and radiated to her limbs, veins and arteries searing with molten hatred. It needed to be controlled. There was no way to extinguish this despicable woman right here at this very moment.

"Why didn't you go to the London Hospital in East End?" Eliza said. "They could have helped you there." Eliza was sure it was because Mary didn't want Sir Jon to find out what she was up to. She wondered what he would do, if anything, were he to discover it.

"They know me too well at that place, if you know what I mean. I wanted to keep things private. Like I told you, it's a gentleman I'm seeing. He'd want me to come here anyhow if he knew. A hospital with lots of women ought to know more about having babies."

"So this gentleman, he doesn't know your plan?" Eliza was pleased she could feign concern, when what she really wanted was to stab her pencil into the woman's eye.

"No, I want to surprise him. Don't look down on me doctor, it's not what you think. He loves me, and he'd be overjoyed if I could give him a baby. He wants one more than anything else in the whole world."

"I see. Well, has everything been working properly down there?"

"Yes."

"And your monthly is regular?"

"Yes."

Eliza couldn't help wondering why Mary even bothered coming to the hospital and was certain it showed on her face.

"I know what you're thinking," she said. "My womanly parts are working fine. I just want to know if there's a way I can get pregnant faster, help it along somehow."

"Ah…well, that's all you had to say." Eliza smiled, her rage buried under miles of cool ice. "There's a new elixir some are using to do what it is you want. It promotes health and optimizes the reproductive system."

"Why haven't I heard of it?"

"Scientists and doctors are just now testing it. I shouldn't have said anything. You must swear to secrecy." Eliza squinted and put her index finger over her lips and whispered, "Shhh."

"Yes, of course," Mary said.

"This hospital is where they are testing it."

"Oh, that's good news. Can I have some then?"

"I'm quite sure you understand they are *very* particular about who gets it."

"Saving it for the rich are they?"

"But maybe…"

"What? Tell me."

"No, it's a silly idea."

"It isn't. Please, you've got to help me."

"Well, every now and again I do charity work at the East End. What if I were to take some from here and bring it to you after I was done with my duties?"

"Or I could just meet you here?"

"No, that won't do. It would give me away for sure if someone saw us talking. It will have to be at night, when I've finished my work. I'll understand if you're too eager and want to look for something else, there are plenty others that would—"

"Don't cut me off, yet. I'm willing to wait. About how long you think?"

"In a week, or two at the latest."

"Well, that's not long at all. I'm up for it."

"Since it will be dark soon, you should probably head back to East End. When I come to see you with the elixir, I'll give you a physical exam then as well if you'd like."

Mary hopped off the table edge. "Such service—who am I to get a personal doctor's visit, and a treatment as well?"

"I feel for your needs. You and your gentleman friend seem desperate for a child."

"Yes doctor, very much so."

"Where shall I come when it's all ready?"

"Miller's Court. Number 13."

"Good. You have your own place?"

"Well, yes. I told you I was seeing a *gentleman*."

"Ah," Eliza said. Sir Jon must be paying for this wench's room. The thought sickened her and the anger swelled again. "I have no way of getting a message to you, so I'll be there when I can. It will be later in the evening, though. That I know."

"I'll be ready."

"Good day to you then, Miss Kelly," Eliza said through gritted teeth.

Mary grabbed Eliza's hand and shook it. "Thank you, doctor. Thank you so much." Then she leaned over, brought it up to her lips and kissed it.

Eliza pulled her hand away. "That's not necessary," she said.

Mary Kelly laughed as she walked out of the partitioned room. It was obvious that she knew she'd made Eliza uncomfortable and was taking advantage.

Behind the makeshift curtain, Eliza clenched the medical papers and held her breath. Feeling faint, she reached over and leaned against the table. Several minutes passed until normalcy came again. She folded up the papers, pushed them into her pocket, then moved the curtain to the side and walked down the hall with a smile across her face.

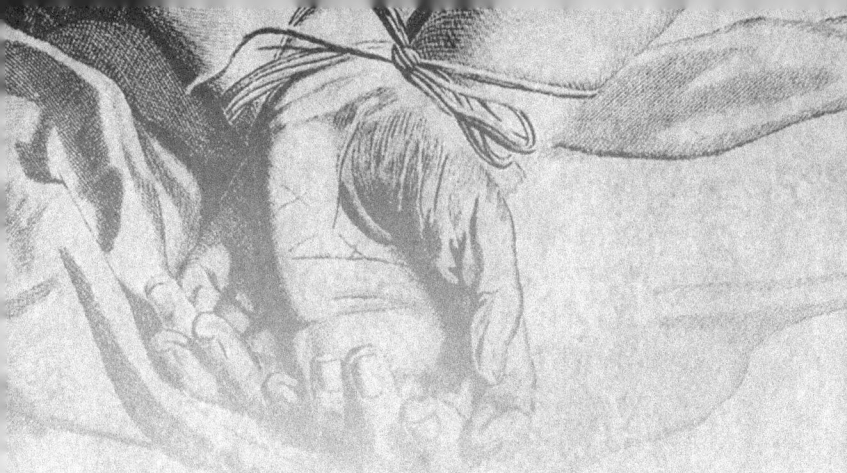

CHAPTER 16

 few days after her encounter with Mary Kelly, Eliza was deeply focused on a dissection of the human heart when Professor Huxley leaned over her shoulder, the odors of liver and onions on his breath. "What is that pinched between your forceps, Miss Covington?" He moved his spectacles down to the tip of his nose.

"A vein, sir." Somewhat startled by him, her words came out more like a question than an answer.

The professor leaned closer to her ear and whispered. "Why bother coming to exams later in the month, you'll only embarrass the both of us, and you're already guaranteed to pass."

"It is a vein, sir," she said with more confidence.

"For what?" He spoke up and straightened his posture.

"The heart."

"But where do they come from?"

Eliza looked up to see if any of her classmates were

watching. They all appeared to be busy with their own dissections. She wondered why he was so particularly hard on her. It seemed brutally unfair.

"Miss Covington," he said.

"Yes."

"Answer the question."

"They're from the body, sir."

"Which part?" He stomped his foot.

Eliza's heart was racing and her cheeks felt warm. She hated Professor Huxley and imagined plunging the forceps into his eyeball then leaving class to the clapping and cheers of the other women.

"The lungs," she said, unsure of her answer.

"Amazing," he said. "And a very lucky guess," he whispered while walking away.

Certain an envious smile was on his face, Eliza wished she could carve a permanent one there. A sense of power surged through her at the thought it was something she could actually make happen. Killing Annie Chapman was an accident, but making it appear as though Jack the Ripper committed the crime was genius—she knew that. Murdering Catherine Eddowes was a choice and she recognized that as well. Eliza had given in to the dark rage she only recently discovered dwelled within her. It was possible to control, but as long as external factors existed triggering the hate, it would need periodic release. Slaying those who hurt her in their roundabout ways as well as those who hurt the ones she loves most, was the only way to liberate the fury.

Eliza arrived home and was removing her hat and gloves when she noticed the day's post on a table in the foyer. A returned letter from Doctor James Riley was on top. Eliza recognized the envelope. "Mrs. Sutton, isn't this one of my wedding invitations?" Eliza picked up the card and showed it to the maid.

"Yes Miss, I believe it is."

"Do you know why one was sent to Doctor Riley?"

"Your mother did the invitations, miss. You'll have to ask her."

"Where is she?"

"In the parlor."

Eliza tossed her frock coat over to Mrs. Sutton, then stormed off with the invitation in her hand. "Mother, what is the meaning of this?" She held the envelope up in the air and waved it back and forth.

Lady Covington looked up from the embroidery work she was doing. "Calm yourself, and don't speak to me that way, it upsets my nerves."

While crossing the room, Eliza noticed the wool skirts worn for school didn't rustle. Perfect for stalking—if she were to tiptoe, no would ever hear her approaching. She held the invitation out for Lady Covington to see.

"What of it?" her mother said.

"Are you taunting him? You know he suffers from a broken heart. How could you?"

"Your father made me send it."

"Why?"

"You should ask him."

"He's been so busy with work these past few evenings, I haven't even seen him."

Lady Covington laughed.

"What do you find amusing about this, Mother?"

"Your father has been spending his evenings at the gentleman's club, dear. And not the ones our circle of friends frequent. Says those detectives and police surgeons come together and work on solving the Whitechapel murders. What do you think of it?"

Eliza kept quiet. *He couldn't possibly be out doing something else—bad things. Not when I'm so close to graduating, marrying, and leaving.*

"Do you believe that's what those men are really doing into the late hours of night? Should I be worried? Eliza, are you listening?"

"Yes, Mother, I mean no, Mother, you shouldn't worry. Father is—"

"I *know* he is knowledgeable and well-respected, but he's not getting any younger and needs his rest."

"I'm going to try and wait up for him tonight. I really want to know why he would send James an invitation. It seems cruel and very unlike Father to do such a thing."

"All men have their reasons for doing what they do. You should leave it alone."

"That's no excuse, and I want an explanation." Eliza tromped out of the parlor.

Eliza waited in her father's study for a long while after dinner. She sat in his desk chair and looked over clipped news articles of the murders, a feeling of guilt soured in the pit of her stomach. Certainly not because there was any reproach for killing the women, but she was to blame for keeping her father working so late at night these past few weeks. He was busy trying to help solve crimes she had committed. Some brandy would surely help the feeling pass, so she poured herself a glass. While taking the occasional sip, her fingers flipped through the pieces of paper, and she read clipped articles from *The Times* in an album Lord Covington made of the murders.

Behind her, on the bookcase wall, were at least a dozen more similar albums he'd put together since her childhood. Eliza was always curious about his fascination with the macabre, but she eventually grew out of it. He'd even handwritten some notes in his latest, *Jack the Ripper* collection. One in particular stood out. Words that were staggered and scrawled out across a page—*"The Juwes are The men That Will not be Blamed for nothing."*

What did it mean? The article on the next page said the chalk writing was on a wall near where they found a piece of bloody apron. Eliza didn't remember seeing the words while cleaning her knife and instruments, but neither was it something she'd been looking for. The bloody apron piece she remembered tossing to the ground. Then she wondered if it were possible that Jack the Ripper had been where she was. Could he have been hiding in a dark corner? Watching her? Eliza was sure she'd have noticed, but maybe not. The Samaritan gentleman came to mind, which made her lift the brandy snifter and take a bigger sip. Was there chalk on his gloves? It was hard to remember.

Looking up to think more on the subject, her father entered the study. "Father," she said. "I'm so glad you're home."

"It's late, Eliza. What could be so important? I'm certain it can wait 'til morning."

Something in his manner exuded a hint of guilt, which had her too perplexed to reply. He came up to the desk, leaned over, and closed the album. Rife with heady cigar smoke and alcohol, her father reeked of a gentleman's club. His strong odor made her step back, and what she saw next made her gasp.

"What is it?" he said.

Eliza looked down at his desk where some scattered newspaper clippings still lay. "Seeing all this death, I think it has affected me."

"It never bothered you before. Take another sip of brandy." While he was collecting the pieces of shorn rectangles and squares, she glanced at his shirt collar again. And there it was—a finger-length's smear of red lipstick. Lord Covington looked up and she turned away.

"You're right, what I wanted to say can wait. I'll talk with you tomorrow." He stepped toward her and leaned in. Repulsed to the point of being faint, it took every bit of her will to kiss him on the cheek. "Good night, Father," she whispered through clenched jaws.

"Get some rest," he said. "You look very out of sorts." He gave her a peck on the cheek.

Wanting to run out of the room, out of the house, and down the street screaming, NO! Eliza forced herself to walk calm and slow out of his study. Instead of going upstairs, she went to the kitchen and poured water from the tea kettle into a basin. Eliza washed her face and lips with scalding water and cried.

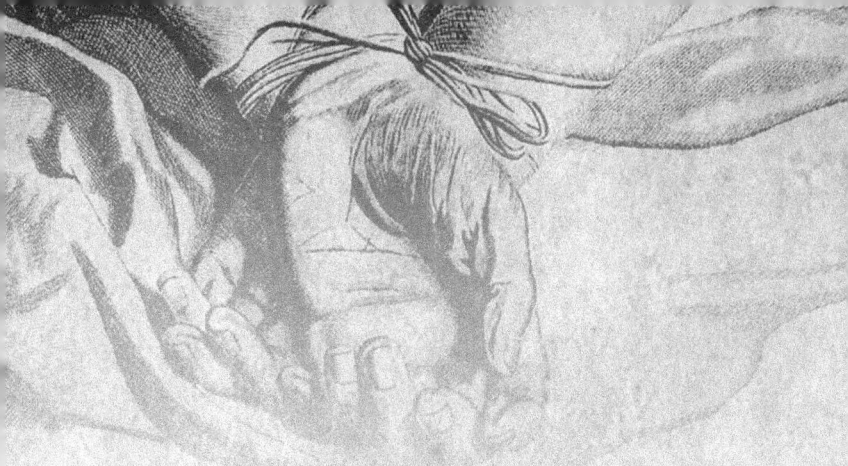

CHAPTER 17

liza's head was in a fog when she woke. Her face felt raw against the crisp linen of the pillow. Flinging back the covers, she got out of bed and inspected her skin in the mirror above the wash basin. It was slightly pink compared to the bright red capillaries webbed across her sclera. Sleep had come late, as dreadful thoughts of the previous night's discovery lingered in her mind and kept her busy thinking, devising. Nanette entered the room to help her get dressed for the day. Without saying a word, she took some powder from the vanity and dabbed it all over Eliza's face.

Downstairs at breakfast, Lord Covington was reading the paper while Lady Covington sipped tea.

"Good morning," her mother said, as Eliza entered the room.

Eliza nodded and smiled.

"You look ill this morning and your eyes are red."

Her father lowered his paper, looked her up and down. "She seems well enough."

"To be in a hospital perhaps," her mother said.

"And that's where I'll be, Mother, so you have nothing to worry about." Eliza pulled out a chair and sat down. Mrs. Sutton came over and poured a cup of tea, then added a splash of milk.

Lady Covington picked up a muffin and tore a piece away with her teeth. After swallowing, she glared at Eliza. "Well, did you talk with your father about the invitation?"

"I—"

"What invitation?" he said.

"The one you had me send James Riley."

"Father, how could you?"

He laughed, shook the newspaper straight and went back to reading.

It was shocking to see this side of him. So heartless and cruel. *An adulterer.* She raised her tea cup between trembling fingers and took a sip. Her mother smirked, and Eliza wondered if she knew and if she did, for how long? *Why hadn't she reacted to it? Had she ever?* It was doubtful. The hate rose, she had to leave. After finishing her last bit of tea, Eliza pushed the plate of uneaten muffin away and stood up.

"Are you leaving?" her mother said. "You've had nothing."

"I'll have something between classes."

Lord Covington didn't say a single word when Eliza left the room.

During one of many tedious lectures by Professor Huxley that day, Eliza wrote Doctor James Riley a letter. It multiplied a hundred times the love she actually felt for him, but she thought he deserved that after how her father had treated him. The note explained why it was impossible for her to return to London Hospital. There was still too much love in her heart for him and it hurt to be near. James would cherish the words and she wondered how long he would keep the letter—maybe forever.

After classes, Eliza made rounds at The Royal Free Hospital on Henrietta Street, since she'd no longer been permitted to go to the London Hospital at East End. Steady traffic came to and from the small supply room where the linen and medicines were kept. Two hours later, mostly everyone charged off to an emergency on the first floor. Eliza quickly walked into the storage room and closed the door. A strong smell of astringent made her wrinkle her nose. Rows of glass bottles and vials lined the shelves. To the right was a cluster of smaller brown vials with droppers. The paper labels on the outside read *laudanum*. Eliza took three of the bottles, wrapped a strip of gauze around each one, and then slipped them into her apron pockets before walking out.

Over the next three days, a total of seven vials were collected, brought home, and their labels removed. But it wasn't until Thursday next, November 8th to be exact, that Eliza carefully lined them upright in her medical bag before leaving the house for classes.

That morning, she'd handed Mrs. Sutton a note with strict directions not to deliver it until dinner. "I won't be dining here tonight," she told the maid, "and I don't want to explain why to Mother just yet."

Mrs. Sutton nodded and took the envelope.

Eliza also left separate instructions with Nanette. "Let them know you saw me in my room and helped me change my clothes. I told you I was dining out with friends and to expect me home late."

"Yes, Miss," Nanette said. When the young maid went back to work, Eliza snuck into the girl's room and stole a black hat from her clothing chest. It was time to give the servant a bit of extra pay for her hard work and to replenish the supply.

With her bag stuffed so full she had to lay her cloak across the top to conceal its contents, Eliza climbed into her family's carriage.

Sitting in class, struggling to stay awake while Professor Huxley lectured on and on about the heart, Eliza thought about graduation exams taking place next week. Feeling confident she would do well— regardless of his hateful remarks about her knowledge or lack thereof—her mind drifted off.

Mary Kelly would be the final victim she'd contribute to the evolution and legacy of Jack the Ripper. Knowing she'd assisted in making the gentleman Samaritan infamous made her smile. Only two days after meeting him, it was resolved in her mind he was most certainly the Whitechapel Murderer— Jack the Ripper as the papers were now calling him. From one killer to another she felt it, the camaraderie of simply knowing the darkness in someone like oneself. Eliza was sure he suspected her as well. He seemed almost protective by telling her not to travel the East End after dark.

By the time she finished classes and rounds at The Royal Free Hospital on Henrietta Street, a dense fog had rolled in on the streets of London. Riding in the hansom made her feel like a normal person again—alive—as though she was going somewhere with a purpose. And what a purpose it was!

After exiting the cab, she put on Nanette's hat. Most of the working girls at East End knew her as Jane by the dark hooded cloak she wore, and she had no want of anyone approaching her for services this evening.

First stop was The London Hospital on Whitechapel Road. Before walking in, she took the letter for James out of her medical bag. Lowering the brim of the hat down over her face, Eliza entered the building. The receptionist was talking to a young couple at her desk. Then she got up from her station and led them somewhere down the hall. Eliza walked over and set the envelope down in plain sight next to some papers, then left. It was time she let James go and moved on with her life. Eliza had familial and social obligations she could not deny. He'd played an important part when she was young and naïve, but that innocence had long since passed.

It was evening and her hunger required some nourishment. In the dark corner of a pub, Eliza sat and ordered a meat pie. Patrons were busy drinking their pints and hardly noticed her. Their conversations revolved around Jack the Ripper, what the police were doing, and that they were a bunch of bumbling idiots.

Darkness blanketed the East End when Eliza walked out of the pub. Intensifying the sinister mood, the fog had gotten much worse. On cold nights as these, thick, black smoke from chimney stacks filled the streets and appeared green against the dim, yellow lamplights. It was an all-encompassing murky haze that included the odor of a bog. She held her gloved hand out and couldn't see it. She smiled, thankful for the perfect situation and felt even more forthright in her plan. It was as if some unknown force was aiding her, making it easier to commit the crime and escape unseen.

Her boots tapped against the cobblestone as she walked. A flat echo of the same sound bounced off a nearby rooftop. It would be difficult to know who or what was coming or going from where. The tapping grew more rapid as she picked up her pace, and soon she would be at Miller's Court knocking on the door of number 13.

This would be a night to remember.

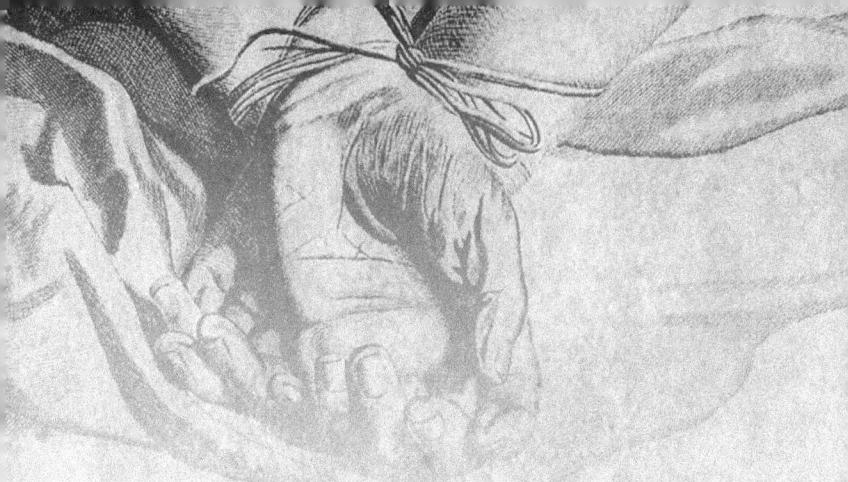

CHAPTER 18

Alleys lined Dorset Street and all the surrounding buildings of Miller's Court. There were almost too many places to choose from for hiding, but Eliza settled on a dark corner across the way from Mary's room. Wanting to be sure the harlot was alone, she watched and waited.

An hour had passed and nothing happened. What if Nanette forgot to tell her mother she was dining with friends? Although, ever since the reigns were handed over for making her wedding arrangements, Lady Covington seemed less worried about where Eliza was or her activities. Lord Covington was out late most nights now. The lipstick on his collar came to mind again and her chest tightened. If it weren't for the detectives and police surgeons dragging him to gentleman's clubs with the excuse of working on the Whitechapel case, he never would have been tempted with adultery. His infidelity was their fault, and she would give those men something to keep them all busy for a while.

Some commotion was taking place outside Miss Kelly's room. The thick haze made it difficult to see. Eliza focused and saw a dark-haired woman with a gaudy red shawl wrapped around her shoulders leaving. Fortunately, it wasn't Miss Kelly. A man was approaching her. "Barnett," she said to him. "What are you doing here?"

"None of your bloody business, now out of my way."

The woman stepped aside and allowed the man access to Mary's room. He opened the door, went in then slammed it behind him. Eliza took in a deep breath and sighed while she watched the woman walk away. It would be a long night. *This particular prostitute stays rather busy.* It was tiring but made her angry enough to continue waiting.

Concealed by the fog, she left the confines of her hiding space and approached Mary's room, crouching down close to a small grimy window. One of the glass panes was broken out and she peeked in. The man, Barrett, had a large build. His physique reminded her of someone who might be a dock worker, and the cap next to his wool trousers with suspenders still attached on the floor reaffirmed it. His wide rear was contracting and relaxing between the whore's legs while he grunted like a pig. Eliza could see nothing else past his mass, and what she was able to observe made her nauseous, so she crept back to her secret hiding place across the way.

It was over two hours later when the man finally left Miss Kelly alone. After waiting another hour to be sure no one else would be coming, Eliza adjusted her hat, picked up her medical bag and approached the building, leery but thankful for the thick vapors that obscured everything.

After pounding on the door with her gloved fist, she took a step back and waited, hoping she gave Mary enough time after her last visitor to wash up. Miss Kelly opened the door wearing a sheer linen chemise and had an expression of curiosity on her face. "Oh yes," she said. "You're the doctor from the Royal Free Hospital. Come in."

Eliza nodded, stepped into the room and waited for Mary to close the door before she spoke. The room was the smallest one she'd ever seen, dark and void of any life or color except for a copy of a famous painting depicting a grieving widow in front of a grave. It was dreadful but felt appropriate. A rank odor of a salty sea hung in the air, along with smoke, and alcohol. It reminded her of what her father smelled like when he came home from the gentleman's club that night.

A small table sat in the corner next to a feeble wooden bed. Centered in the room against the far wall was the fireplace, the surrounding bricks stained by the black of burnt cinder and ash. An old table and two chairs were positioned in front of it. "Are you expecting anyone?" Eliza said, biting her tongue and stopping short of a longer question. She nearly added the word *else* at the end which might have triggered some suspicion.

Walking toward the fire, really only five steps into the room, she noticed Mary's undergarment hanging over the back of a seat. Eliza took off her hat and hung it on the chair's wooden post, inadvertently concealing most of the shoddy clothing. Not wanting to put her bag on the table, she placed it on the same chair as her hat, and then opened it. One by one, she took out the unmarked vials of laudanum. Mary joined her at the table with her eyes wide and a smile on her face at the sight of the small glass bottles. "You really came through, Miss," the harlot said. "When should I take it? Shall I have some now?"

"Yes, yes, I'm getting to that."

"You still doing a bodily exam?"

"I think it would be a good idea, don't you?"

"Let me just wash up a bit."

Acidic bile rose up Eliza's throat and burned the back of her palate and tonsils. She quickly swallowed hard to make it go back down. Mary went over to the wash basin on the table next to the bed and dropped a piece of fabric into the water. Lifting up her chemise with one hand, she then took the wet cloth with the other and squeezed the excess liquid, then began vigorously wiping between her legs. Eliza swallowed another wave of rising stomach acid, then turned away and looked deep into her medical bag. The metallic blade of the surgical knife reflected the orange glow from the fire. She reached in, grabbed hold of the handle, and lifted the instrument so that it was resting at the very top of the bag. Ignoring what Mary was still doing, Eliza walked over to the bed and set the bag down at the foot of it and off to the right.

Mary had finished cleaning herself and followed behind Eliza as they both walked over to the table. The liquid in the brown glass vials appeared to dance with the flames of the fire behind them, captivating and hypnotizing the prostitute. Eliza smiled, thinking this would be too easy. "You'll want to drink one whole bottle a day until they're all gone," she said. "Then in the next week or so, your body should be primed for reproduction."

Mary snatched one of the bottles off the table and removed the stopper. Then she circled the vial's opening under her nose. "Smells awful strong, almost like—"

"Drink it," Eliza said. Her heart began to race as she watched the prostitute put the glass to her lips, tip the entire bottle of laudanum into her mouth, then swallow it all in one gulp.

"Ack!" The prostitute gagged.

"Quick, put your head back," Eliza shouted. "Don't you dare spit that up!"

Mary coughed, then caught her breath and calmed. "It's a worse bitter than laudanum that." She stared at the bottle before setting it back down on the table.

"Nothing of the sort, stop exaggerating. Do you want to get pregnant or not?"

"Aye, Miss."

"Besides, it's only for a week. Can you do it, or shall I leave this minute and take it with?"

Mary slowly nodded her head with a ridiculous smile across her face. Eliza wondered if the opium was already at work.

"Have you eaten recently?" she asked Mary.

"Not since breakfast." She laughed and swooned a little to the left.

"Excellent, then let's get on with that exam."

As the prostitute stumbled over to the bed, a hint of sympathy touched Eliza to see such a pathetic creature. Mary was a pretty girl with blue eyes almost like her own. They were both young and already set on their paths by unseen hands that forced them along an invisible board, like game pieces. There was no changing who would win; in the end she knew it would be the men. In that moment, Eliza decided she wouldn't kill the poor wretch. Simply do the world a favor and make having children for her impossible.

Mary sat on the side of the bed just in time, a second later, and she might have hit the floor. Eliza picked her legs up by the ankles and swung them around onto the bed. The rest of her body fell back against the flimsy mattress of straw and fabric. She lay there and began laughing.

"You'll need to stop moving for the exam," Eliza said.

The prostitute nodded, then put her hands over her mouth, but continued to giggle. A candle stuck into a broken wine bottle was situated on the bedside table. Shaking off the nonsense, Eliza stepped over and got it, then brought the light closer to where she would be working. She rolled the sleeves of her cloak and frock coat then raised Mary's chemise over her hips, exposing the pale skin around the pink flesh of her vaginal opening. A small triangular patch of fine blonde-reddish pubic hair was right above it, reminding Eliza of Greco-Roman paintings depicting beautiful nude women.

Mary instinctively spread her legs apart and Eliza was not repulsed by what she saw. It was one of the lovelier specimens she'd ever seen. Finding it hard to concentrate, she could do nothing but stare.

"Well," Mary said. Taking Eliza's eyes away from the piece of heaven so many men adored.

"I don't see anything significant on the outside." "That's good isn't it?"

"Yes, but I need to get a look within." Eliza put her hands on Mary's legs and gently pushed them back. "Hold them like that," she told the girl. Then Eliza positioned herself on her knees at the end of the small bed. Leaning forward didn't take much, and then she was right between Mary's legs. Despite the nasty dock worker who had recently been there, the scent that wafted up onto Eliza's face was clean and almost sweet. It was apparent why this girl in particular was so busy and had a gentleman keeping her. Then she remembered why she was there. The man Mary spoke of didn't deserve to be trapped, not that way anyhow, and as busy as this whore was selling her beautiful wares, Eliza would never have to worry about her needing any backstreet abortion services when she was through with her.

"You'll feel some pressure." She plunged her index and middle finger inside Mary as far back as they would go. With her other hand on top of the prostitute's abdomen she simultaneously pushed down and pushed up her fingers, feeling the organs in between.

Mary groaned a little, but it wasn't a sound of discomfort. Eliza thought the woman might actually be enjoying it. She looked down at her face and her eyes were closed, but her lips made a slight smile. Through her sheer chemise, Eliza saw her erect nipples along with her firm round breasts, which were nearly as perfect as what was between her legs. She adjusted her fingers inside a little and watched a kind of ecstasy veil Mary's face. The woman moved her rear end up in circles and Eliza felt her vaginal walls clench. Moisture that was warm and soft filled the cavity. Eliza slid her fingers out and observed the clear glistening substance. Mary's eyes were still closed. She was heavy under the influence of the laudanum and Eliza knew she could do anything to her with little protest.

After wiping the glazed fingers on the bed, she reached back into her bag and fished for the long curette. Mary started giggling again.

"Stop moving," Eliza said.

Eyes still closed, she sighed softly. "You did that nearly as well as my gentleman friend."

"Don't try and turn a simple exam into a loathsome act." Eliza was flushed with anger and embarrassment, so she spoke her mind, assuming the prostitute probably wouldn't remember the conversation. "Sir Jon should be spending his time with his wife. Not with the likes of you."

The prostitute's laughter intensified, shaking the entire bed. Eliza's heart began to race and pound. The high pitch made her head throb. "Stop laughing," she shouted. "There's nothing funny about it."

Mary paused for a moment, a huge drug-induced smile across her face. Then she said, "Sir Jon isn't my *particular* gentleman, Miss Doctor." More laughing came and then panting for air in between. "He's one of my favorites, but no, it's Lord Covington I'm all about."

Eliza stopped breathing. Her vision blackened from the periphery inward. With one hand still in the medical bag fumbling for the curette, a sudden sharp sting and then an itch came from her pinky finger. The pain kept the darkness from blinding her completely. It was the surgical knife. She carefully slid her fingers along the flat of the blade until she reached the handle. Then she pulled it from the bag.

The drugged whore's eyes were still closed when Eliza turned toward her. The laughing had become taunting cackling. With the instrument in her hand, Eliza moved over

Mary's spread legs, which the prostitute still held back with her hands. Before losing her sight to the blackness that was quickly closing in, Eliza thought of a backhand stroke. She threw an imaginary ball up into the air, and moved her arm back. Mary opened her eyes and Eliza swung.

It was the hardest game of lawn tennis she'd ever played, and it all happened in the dark. A heart-pumping frenzy of swinging and striking that required all her energy, and hate was the fuel. Her vision came back in flashes—images of blue eyes staring up at her, blood, and gore.

Eliza wasn't quite finished with the game. She continued to play until her sight had fully returned. What she saw was annihilation, but to her, still incomplete, not done. Mary's lifeless head turned toward the wall. "Don't you look away, Miss Kelly," Eliza said to the mutilated corpse. She took a large piece of flesh she'd cut away and what looked to be an organ and propped them under the body's head to keep it straight. Mary appeared to be watching what Eliza was doing which was what she wanted.

"You desired to have a baby with my father. Here, right?" She cleared out the rest of the young woman's innards and then put her lifeless hand in the empty cavity. "It may be a little difficult for you now. And to think I was going to let you live. You have no heart, Mary Kelly. No heart at all." Eliza gripped the knife handle with both hands, raised it up in the air and plunged it down into the middle of the body's chest. Then she moved the blade back and forth to pry the sternum apart. When there was a large enough opening she pulled the rest of the ribcage apart with her bare hands. Bone shards cut into her palms, but she hardly noticed.

The heart was still warm when Eliza extracted it, wrapped it in a swatch of fabric, then placed it down into her bag. Sitting up on her knees, she realized her clothing was drenched in blood and bits of bone, flesh, and hair. Piece by piece, she removed her clothing and placed them into the fire. Because the wool was damp, it was necessary to stoke up the flames and add a log or two to get it nice and hot and keep it that way until every blood-stained garment was ash. In her frenzy, she'd sliced her arms and thighs. Fortunately, her skirts had taken most of the slashes to her legs. The ones on her forearms were a little deeper but wouldn't need stitches.

Another piece of bed linen was torn away to wipe her knife off before putting it away. Careful not get any more blood on herself, she went over to the water basin, dipped one end of a clean piece of linen into the bowl then quickly yanked it out, assuring her no blood would get in the water.

The hearth was ablaze and lit up the room even better than daylight. Eliza noticed the broken window pane as she looked around. There was an extra piece of linen she crumpled up in her hand and set into the open frame. Just in case someone walking by did the same thing she'd done earlier and peeked in.

All that was left clean was her chemise and a layer of underskirt. Eliza picked up the broken wine bottle that held the burning candle and looked around the dark corners of the room for clothes. Mary's green bodice and brown skirt was what she found and quickly put on. There was also a shawl

Eliza picked up and wrapped around her head and shoulders to partially cover her face. One more time, she went around the room and gathered up what was hers. About to walk out the door with her medical bag discreetly tucked under her arm and hidden by the shawl, she saw the hat. Eliza walked over, picked it up and put it on top of the blazing fire. She looked back at Mary's body, whose head had turned to face the wall again.

Not only had Jack the Ripper evolved.

He had become the perfect killer.

CHAPTER 19

The following day was the Lord Mayor's Show, complete with a parade and multiple celebrations to honor the newly-elected Sir James Whitehead. The festivities were in full procession by noon. Eliza slept in, knowing her family never attended the parade. Lady Covington refused to stand out in the dreary November weather for anyone. The Covingtons would honor this year's elected official by attending the dinner held by the Royal Courts later in the evening.

Before sitting down to breakfast, Eliza stepped over to the window above the sideboard, pulled a curtain open and looked outdoors. A befitting air of gloom came from the sea in the guise of dark ashen clouds. Even cold, wet weather wouldn't keep the throngs of people, desperate for something to celebrate, in their warm homes, and soon the news of another murder would be spreading through London streets faster than the plague.

Eliza knew they would not be making the Royal Dinner this year. She visualized her father in his study with his head hung low, emptying his brandy decanter, asking for another, while grieving over his dead whore. He would get over it soon enough. Eliza had done a great service for all those whom she cared deeply about.

Now Mary Kelly's heart was nothing but ash settled at the bottom of her family's kitchen's hearth. Soon to be shoveled out by Mr. Sutton and put into the trash, which will eventually make its way into the Thames, and once more end up at the East End where she belonged.

Life in the Covington house during the next three weeks, played out exactly as Eliza had imagined. Throughout the rest of November, her father spent most evenings alone in his study. Lady Covington carried on as though nothing had happened, although she did seem somewhat merrier than she had been before.

Just as Professor Huxley had confidentially told her, Eliza graduated from the London School of Medicine for Women. No honors were given, of course, but she hardly cared anymore. What she'd learned about herself and the human body elevated her status above and beyond the classical education.

Inspector Abberline congratulated Eliza at the graduation dinner her parents hosted at the end of the month. "And thank you for your past advice with...Whitechapel," he said.

"Have you any new leads?" she inquired.

The inspector looked over at Lord Covington who was standing across the room near the punch bowl with his head hung low. "No miss, none whatsoever—nothing for you to worry about, though. Best of luck with your nuptials next month and then off to America, I hear?"

"Yes, sir," Eliza said. Henry was standing by her side smiling from ear to ear.

"Blessings to you both." Inspector Abberline nodded then walked off toward Lord Covington and the two men spoke quietly to one another, looking around the room for anyone who might be watching. Eliza wasn't concerned. She knew they were proud, educated men, chasing their tails. As she'd overheard once in the East End pub, 'they were bumbling idiots.'

Then it was a great surprise to all the guests when Ann Williams and her husband entered the room. Eliza quickly walked up and shook hands with her. While Henry spoke to Sir Jon, Eliza led Ann over to the table covered in seasonal sweets and delights.

"I never thanked you," Ann said softly.

"Please, there's no need. You would've done the same for me. Things are better for you at home, I think." Eliza looked deep into Ann's eyes.

"Yes, much, thank you again."

"And how was the eating chocolate? All these glorious treats spread out as far as the eye can see and not a single chocolate. I've yet to convince Father it isn't an evil thing."

"Speaking of evil things," Ann swallowed and looked down at the floor. "You don't know anything about the latest Whitechapel murder, do you?"

"Nothing at all, but what luck, right?"

"Eliza," Ann whispered as if to shush her.

"What is it, Ann? You can't tell me you're not happy with the news. You look absolutely beautiful this evening."

Ann was about to say something more, but Eliza waved Henry and Sir Jon over.

"What is it dear?" Henry said. He handed her a glass full of bubbling champagne.

"I was just telling Ann how absolutely beautiful she looks this evening. Don't you think so, Henry?"

"Yes, of course." He smiled at her, raised his champagne glass and took a sip.

"Wouldn't you agree as well, Sir Jon? Ann's beauty this evening rivals anything else that ever came out of Wales."

Sir Jon coughed and cleared his throat. His face turned red and Henry patted him on the back. "Are you all right?" he asked him.

"Yes, I'm fine. I'm fine."

"Well, I suppose," Henry said. "If you were to become ill, a room full of doctors would be the place to do it."

Sir Jon agreed and everyone laughed except for Ann. She stared at Eliza with squinted eyes. Once more she was about to speak, when Sir Jon took her by the arm, excused their leaving, then led her over to Lady Covington.

Henry turned to face Eliza, leaned in, and kissed her on the cheek. "Ah my dear, I'm so proud you've succeeded in this accomplishment I know you've been wanting."

"I am so happy."

"I'm sure our joy will only continue with the wedding and our move."

"Henry?" Eliza stepped back so that she could look him in the eyes.

"What is it? You upset about leaving? I know—"

"America's such a big country, Henry. Must we be always confined to New York City?"

Henry smirked. "Of course not, dear. Father has plans to open banks across the entire country. We'll be traveling from one coast to the other and you shall see *all* of America. And I'm almost certain every place we reside will be in need of an educated doctor."

Sudden images of Henry between the legs of American whores flashed through her mind, and she immediately tightened her grip around the glass. Before it shattered in her hand, Eliza remembered the way she'd left Mary Kelly. The prostitute's helpless, dead stare with those pale blue eyes in an unrecognizable face released the tension in her hold.

Eliza smiled and raised the glass to him.

"To new beginnings."

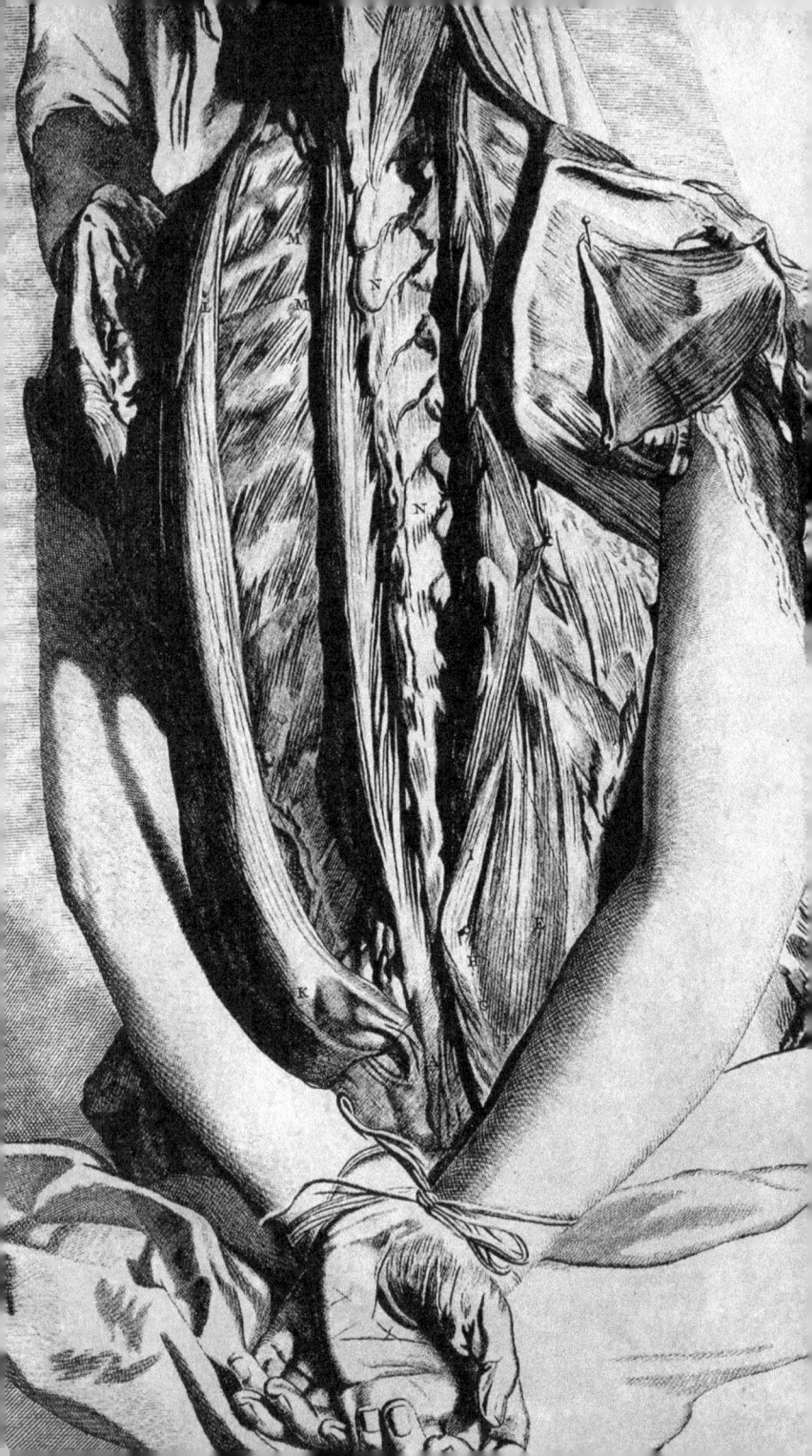

ACKNOWLEDGMENTS

A big thanks to Gene O'Neill and Gord Rollo, the "Burke and Hare" of horror writers, Alan M. Clark, Norman Rubenstein, JG Faherty, and Chris Marrs.

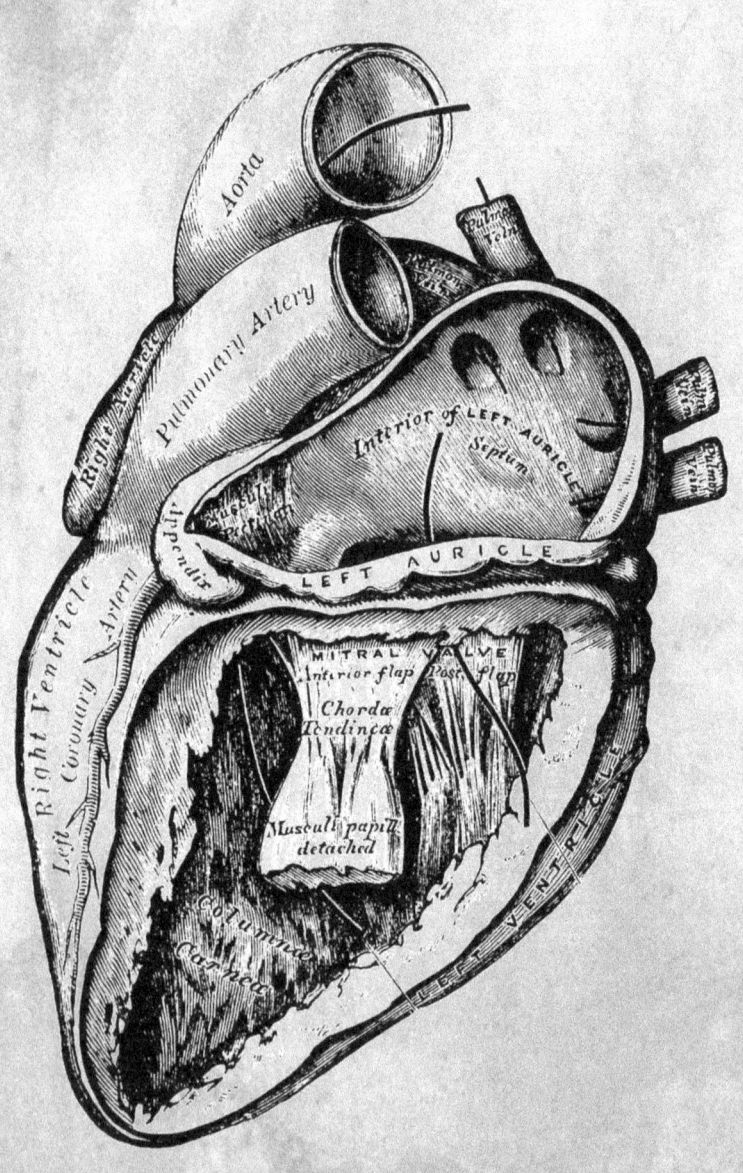

ABOUT THE AUTHOR

Rena Mason is the Bram Stoker Award® winning author of *The Evolutionist* and *East End Girls*. A longtime fan of horror, sci-fi, science, history, historical fiction, mysteries, and thrillers, she began writing to mash up those genres in stories revolving around everyday life.

She is a member of the Horror Writer's Association, Pacific Northwest Writer's Association, and International Thriller Writers. She writes a column for the HWA Monthly Newsletter, "Recently Born of Horrific Minds" and writes occasional articles. She also does volunteer work for the Horror Writer's Association.

An avid SCUBA diver since 1988, she has traveled the world and enjoys incorporating the experiences into her stories.

Currently, she resides in Las Vegas, Nevada with her family.